AN IRON HAND

"If the Englishman is not found and handed over to us by one o'clock today," Staudt shouted, "twelve prisoners will be shot. The first dozen will include your Mayor, town officer, and other municipal staff presently in our custody."

Subdued uproar; a gnarled old man close to the steps shook his fist and howled. Raging, a fat woman in a canvas apron waddled toward the tank only to be pounced on by two soldiers and dragged bodily away.

"At three o'clock," Staudt went on, "twenty more, prisoners will be executed. Twenty selected at random. At five o'clock, thirty more, and so on until the Englishman is surrendered."

Wailings, cries of rage and terror rose up from the throng. The soldiers snapped rifled bolts and aimed into the swaying crowd.

THE FIGHTING SAGA OF THE
SAS
BOOK 1: WARRIOR CASTE

JAMES ALBANY

PINNACLE BOOKS NEW YORK

This novel is a work of fiction. Names, characters, places, and
incidents are either the product of the author's imagination or are
used fictitiously. Any resemblance to actual events or places or
persons, living or dead, is entirely coincidental.

THE FIGHTING SAGA OF THE SAS BOOK 1: WARRIOR CASTE

Copyright © 1982 by James Albany

A Pinnacle Books edition, published by special arrangement with
Pan Books Ltd.

Pan edition published in 1982
Pinnacle edition/April 1985

ISBN: 0-523-42520-1

Printed in the United States of America

PINNACLE BOOKS, INC.
1430 Broadway
New York, New York 10018

9   8   7   6   5   4   3   2   1

Contents

We may feel sure that nothing of which we have any knowledge or record has ever been done by mortal men which surpasses the splendor and daring of their feats of arms.

—Winston S. Churchill

Although Special Air Service did not achieve formal regimental status until August 1942, the first intake of recruits had already experienced warfare on the lonely margins of military life, in Finland, Norway, in the Western Desert and in France. Culled from all sorts of units and task forces, "mobs" hastily pulled together to carry the fight against Nazi oppression behind enemy lines, its troops possessed certain qualities in common, courage, stamina and daring being chief among them.

Lieutenant Deacon, Sergeant Campbell and Corporal McNair did not, to my knowledge, have exact counterparts in reality, yet they typify that breed of soldier later forged into the world's most feared fighting force.

—James Albany

WARRIOR CASTE

1 Death of a virgin

AT A QUARTER PAST SIX on an overcast morning towards the end of May 1940, SS Obergruppenführer Josef Ribbeck drove into the little French town of St. Félice.

The general sat alone in the rear compartment of an armored Mercedes sedan chauffeured by a blond corporal in a tailored gray uniform. Ribbeck revelled in the company of handsome boys and, to the chagrin of his senior officers, insisted on surrounding himself with *lieblings* chosen more for their looks than their intelligence.

The flag of the Nazi eagle was masted on the hood of the Mercedes and on its sweeping wings a commander's gold-embroidered pennant and the shield and skull of the SS Panzer Division Totenkopf snapped stiffly in the breeze. Heavy-duty tires thundered on the cobbles and the big supercharged 200 bhp engine roared as the car swept towards the town hall where Sturmbann-führer Eric Staudt waited, nervously, for the general's arrival.

The major had no reason to be nervous. Staudt was an officer of the "old school" who had served in the SS since its inception. His loyalty to the regiment was unquestioned and he had carried out the general's commands to the letter; St. Félice had been secured and sealed, sealed so tightly that a mouse could not leave or enter unchallenged.

Staudt had pulled two half-companies out of the assault zone to defend the town's sprawling periphery. Roadblocks had been established, sentries posted on neighboring farms and patrols in the woods. In the bullring east of the railway station a dozen light tanks were leaguered and Allied resistance had been cleared from the Rue de St. Félice as far west as the Quern canal.

In all, over two hundred SS fighting men were poised to carry out the Obergruppenführer's commands, whatever those commands might be.

For all that, Staudt remained nervous. The presence of the girl in the first-floor office made him tense. He could not fathom why SS Obergruppenführer Ribbeck would go to so much trouble to lay hands on a pretty nineteen-year-old French librarian who, as far as Staudt could deduce, was innocent of any crime against the Reich.

When Staudt heard the chop of boot-heels on the town hall's worn steps and the clash of guards' rifles he hastily ground out his cigarette, fastened his tunic collar and squared his cap. As Ribbeck strode in through the open door the Sturmbannführer saluted and wished the general a good morning.

Sourly Ribbeck returned the salute, shucked off his greatcoat, tossed it to a chair, closed the door with his elbow and swung to face the major.

"Do you have the female under lock and key?"

"Yes, Herr General. In the office next door."

At forty-seven, Ribbeck emanated bull-like confidence. Cropped hair was peppered with gray above close-set ears. He had a blunt jaw and a hooked nose that the propaganda press had likened to the beak of a mountain eagle, an analogy that might have been accurate before a police baton shattered it in a street fight during the Munich Beer Hall *putsch* twenty years ago.

"Was she difficult to track down?" Ribbeck asked.

"No, Herr General. She was in the library. We took her late last night, without a struggle."

"Was she alone?"

"Completely alone."

"I assume you searched the building."

"Throughly."

"How quickly was the town secured?"

"By noon yesterday. The first and second battalions of the Leibstandarte had the honor of fighting. By the time we arrived the British brigades had fallen back into the Wormhout sector. All we had to do was mop up. There were no casualties."

"Did you take prisoners?"

"Four Britishers."

"Were any wounded?"

"No, Herr General."

"Where are they now?"

"Under guard at Melampyre Farm, a couple of miles away on the edge of the town, together with the dignitaries and other hostiles on your list."

"He cannot possibly have escaped?"

"No, sir. No man, woman or child has been permitted to leave. And no man, woman or child has entered the area. I have a motorcycle unit patrolling the road to Quern and traffic, including the passage of prisoners and refugees, has been diverted. The Luftwaffe are cooperating in keeping the corridor open."

"You have done well, Staudt."

"Thank you, sir."

Ribbeck crossed to the window, lifted the net curtain and stared down into the street.

Pale sunlight had struggled through the dawn cloud. On a normal day the street would have been alive with produce-carts. Bakers' shops would have been unshuttered and the appetizing aroma of hot loaves would have infiltrated the dusty corridors of the town hall. Today, though, the street was like the grave. Staudt's curfew was still in operation. The citizens of St. Félice, friends and enemies alike, were prisoners in their homes.

Ribbeck turned. "Bring me the girl, Staudt."

The major hesitated. "May I ask, sir, why the girl is so important to the Totenkopf?"

"She is not important to the Totenkopf," said Ribbeck. "She is, however, important to the Reich. At least, the man she helped to hide is important. It is that man we have been instructed to find and take alive."

"Is he a general?"

"No, he is an English doctor of science, a leading world expert in radio location systems." Understanding brightened Staudt's bewilderment as Ribbeck went on. "This doctor, Philip Paget, was lured out of England into a trap set for him by our Intelligence Service, with the active collusion of a french professor, an admirer of the Führer, who is even now on his way to Berlin. The British were fools to allow Paget to walk into the trap. But, by luck, Paget

evaded capture in Lille. The plane in which he was escaping was
brought down near here."

"Yesterday?"

"In the early hours of the morning, yes."

"But why were we, a fighting regiment, summoned to find
him?"

"The Leibstandarte were committed to another attack and,
having taken St. Félice without much effort, Sepp Dietrich insisted
that they be permitted to march on. As a personal favor to the
Führer—who is keenly interested in what Paget can tell us about
the British RDF system—I agreed to perform the chore. But I have
no intention of loitering, Staudt. I want to be out of here, heading
for Quern by mid-afternoon, if not before, with Paget on his way
back to Germany for interrogation."

"Of course, Herr General."

"Paget is in the hands of a local resistance group, communists
who persist in defying us. But we too have our allies, our
informants, which is the reason we know that Paget is wounded
and cannot be whisked away without risk."

"A search of the area will flush him out."

"Do not be so sure, Staudt. This miserable town covers many
acres and it was not, as you will have noticed, much battered by
the guns. One man could be hidden here for weeks. However, I am
sure that the girl will tell us where Paget may be found."

"The girl seems stubborn, sir."

"She will not remain stubborn for long. Bring her in, Staudt,
immediately."

"Yes, Herr General."

Staudt had put the girl under guard in an anteroom of the Clerk
of Works' office, a bleak chamber with a bench and table and no
other furniture. Bread and milk that Staudt had provided for the
prisoner's breakfast remained untouched. The girl was seated on
the bench, hands in her lap. Her knees were pressed together and
her head was lowered modestly. She appeared, to Staudt, utterly
defenseless. He felt a wave of sympathy for her plight.

The two privates who had been ordered to watch over her
clicked to attention when Staudt entered. The major had no doubt
that they had enjoyed themselves during the night, baiting the girl.

The soldiers were young and arrogant and regarded everything in skirts as fair game for the élite of the SS Totenkopf.

When Staudt called out her name, the girl looked up. He was surprised that there was no fear in her eyes, only a passive defiance that made Staudt anxious on her behalf. She wore a white shirt blouse, a brown skirt and low-heeled shoes. She had the neatness, the simple style, of a country girl and reminded Staudt of an instructress in French with whom he had fallen madly in love when he was ten years old and a pupil in the Aachen Volksschule. She also reminded him of his daughters at home in Roseheim, though they were younger.

SS Sturmbannführer spoke excellent French. He requested that the mademoiselle accompany him into the adjoining room.

Unhesitatingly the girl rose and preceded the major into the Clerk of Works' office. Staudt told the privates to remain where they were and closed the connecting door.

In a pool of sunlight by the Clerk's deal chart table the Obergruppenführer waited, hands on hips. He looked aggressive, almost savage.

Staudt's fears for the girl grew. He wished that he was elsewhere, in the mess, riding a *panzerwagen*, commanding a tank corps in a massed assault, anywhere that an SS major belonged, not here in rural France co-opted into torturing a child.

In halting French, Ribbeck said, "Are you Lisa Vandeleur?"

"Yes, I am Lisa Vandeleur."

"Do you speak the German language?"

"I speak French," said the girl. "And English."

"Tell her to look at me," said Ribbeck to Staudt.

Staudt relayed the general's instruction.

The girl raised her gaze to Ribbeck's face and met his scrutiny with a calmness that even the general, who was not noted for sensitivity, recognized as obstinacy. The Obergruppenführer's obsessional impatience to be quit of this chore and return to fighting was not appeased. His thin lips compressed, whitening, then he told Staudt to ask the girl where she had hidden the English scientist.

Staudt put the question in rapid French.

"I know nothing of an English scientist," the girl replied.

Staudt reminded her that she was in serious peril and that it would be better for her if she cooperated.

"I know nothing of an English scientist," the girl repeated.

Ribbeck caught the drift of her reply.

"Tell her if she takes us to the Englishman she will be released at once."

Staudt translated the general's offer.

"I do not know where the Englishman is hidden."

"She claims she does not know where—"

"Tell her she has my word as a German officer that she will be released unharmed."

The girl smiled slightly. "What is the word of a German officer worth these days?"

Staudt said quickly, "It is not the promise but the threat you should heed, young woman. Tell us where the Englishman is hidden. Nobody need know that you gave us the information. In two or three weeks, when the English are crushed, everybody in France will be our friend."

"What are you saying, Staudt?"

"I'm reasoning with her, Herr General."

"We will do the Englishman no physical harm, I assure you, ma'mselle," Staudt continued. "It is imperative, however, that the man is prevented from returning to his own country. You are not a child. You must understand that we cannot let him go."

"I do not know what you are talking about," the girl said.

"She claims she knows nothing, sir."

"I expected as much. Very well. Remove her skirt."

"Herr General?"

"Take off her skirt, Staudt."

"Sir, the Hague Convention expressly prohibits the—"

"Do not teach me the rules of war," Ribbeck hissed. "The rules of war are for politicians and cowards, not soldiers."

"Allow me to reason with her once more, sir."

"God in Heaven, are you squeamish?"

"When it comes to this sort of thing, sir, I do not approve."

"The SD are crying out for officers to staff their political detention centers. Perhaps you would prefer to be transferred to a post at Dachau and practice the rules of war there."

"I am not a security guard, sir. I am a fighting soldier."

"In that case, the quicker you obey me the quicker we will get the job done and return to fighting a proper enemy. Take off her skirt and underclothes. Sit her upon the table."

Color drained from the girl's face. Her skin was almost translucent, like the petals of a lily. She had understood the general's order and what it implied.

Kneeling, Strumbannführer Staudt clumsily unbuttoned the skirt. Though she was outwardly calm, Staudt's fingers detected a telltale trembling in the girl's thighs. The skirt slid to the floor. She stepped out of it. Now Staudt was obliged to remove a half-slip and a pair of white cotton knickers. In spite of her slenderness the girl's body was womanly and mature. When she was unclad from the waist down, Staudt gently took her elbow, steered her to the chart table and indicated that she should sit upon it.

Ribbeck moved close. In abominable French he said, "I will give you one more opportunity to tell me where you have hidden the Englishman."

Staudt began to translate but the girl interrupted,

In halting German she spoke directly to Ribbeck. "I do not know where the Englishman is hidden—and if I did I would not tell you."

Ribbeck sighed theatrically. "Ach, what a shame that is."

Staudt would never forget the next few minutes, though many other brutal acts would be laid over the memory in the course of the war that was to come.

The Obergruppenführer lifted his greatcoat from the chair by the door. While the girl and the major watched in puzzlement the general fished in the deep pocket and brought out an oilcloth pouch fastened with a rubber band. He tossed the coat down again and walked back to the table, snapping the band on the pouch and unwrapping the oilskin as he came.

Staudt had seen no gun quite like it; a toy, an ugly toy, the primitive breechblock riding slots on the end of a stubby barrel. Carefully Ribbeck drew the enlarged cocking piece to the rear and stroked the firing pin rod which jutted out.

"An interesting weapon, is it not, Staudt?"

"Sir?"

"A new model developed at the Lichputze laboratories in Garmisch, tested but not yet on general issue."

"What—what sort of weapon is it?" Staudt asked.

"A flare projector, of course. Pocket size. It will soon be supplied to our airborne divisions for use in the field. Smoothbore, single shot." Ribbeck took a cartridge from the pouch, a .45 calibre topped with an inch-long case of red pasteboard, like a shotgun shell. "The flare is here, you see; a stable chemical compound containing phosphorous. It has an arc height of two hundred feet and a visible range of two miles. Useful, don't you think?"

"In the field, sir, yes."

"And elsewhere." Ribbeck inserted the cartridge. "It is also designed to serve as an incendiary device at short range. When pressed against a surface—thus—the soft head disperses flame laterally."

As he spoke, the Obergruppenführer opened the girl's knees and pressed the pistol's muzzle against her pubic mound just above the delta of soft dark hair.

The girl flinched and wriggled and Ribbeck looped his left arm about her shoulders, holding her still.

"Now, fräulein, where have you hidden the Englishman?"

"I . . . do . . . not . . . know."

"You have ten seconds to give me the information—"

Staudt began to translate but Ribbeck cut him off, saying. "She understands me well enough."

Ribbeck tightened his hold, bending her body backward. Her long legs stuck out. One shoe dangled from her toes. Her arms were pressed about the general's shoulder, fingers raking the gray cloth.

"If you do not tell me, I will be obliged to test this interesting new weapon. Upon you."

Staudt could no longer see the snout of the pistol. Pain and humiliation were scribbled all over the girl's face.

"Tell me, you bitch," said Ribbeck, thickly.

The gesture was so sudden and unexpected that neither man had a chance to react. The girl's hands flailed, than found their targets and snapped over the general's elbows. She jerked his arms violently towards her and at the same instant spat into his eyes.

The flare gun discharged with a loud rush.

Tendrils of red and yellow flame engulfed the girl and the general, and Ribbeck cried out and pitched himself away from her, flinging her back upon the table where she writhed, shrieking, as the chemical ate into her flesh.

Ribbeck pranced about the room, beating at the flame stains that speckled his tunic, bawling for Staudt to help him.

Staudt slung the greatcoat around the commander and hugged it with his arms, smothering the burning then, leaving the general to attend to himself, leapt towards the mutilated girl.

She was beyond his aid, far into dying. Her features were calm and composed once more, but her torso was hideous, slick and blistered and carbon-black. Putting his arm about her, Staudt supported her head.

"God in Heaven," he muttered. "What have you done?"

Life ebbed out of the dark eyes. There was nothing he could do, nothing at all. Then he noticed the tiny gold crucifix on a chain about her throat and quickly placed it on her parted lips. She smiled at him faintly—or was it only the first neat rictus of death?

"The bitch," Ribbeck was shouting. "The ignorant Jew-bitch."

With the greatcoat clapped about his waist the Obergruppen-führer tried to push Staudt aside, to get at the girl, to punish her corpse for having denied him his will.

But Staudt would not give way.

"She wasn't a Jew," he said.

"Why then did she do it? Tell me that, Staudt. Why did she do it?"

Staudt could not, at that moment, give Ribbeck an answer.

An hour later, however, a hysterical Frenchwoman was brought before the commander to plead, too late, for her daughter's life.

Staudt was allotted the task of escorting the woman to the basement where the girl's body, wrapped in a clean army blanket, had been taken. It was laid out upon a mattress on a table under a naked light bulb.

"It was an accident, madame." Staudt supported the bereft mother. "I assure you that the army was not responsible."

The woman was in shock. "Sylvie. Ma petite Sylvie," she crooned, rocking against the major. Though muffled by sobs and not distinct, the words were clear enough to catch Staudt's attention.

"What, madame, was your daughter's name?" he inquired gently.

"Sylvie. Sylvie Fromont."

"She wasn't Lisa Vandeleur?"

"No, no. She was my daughter. Her name was Sylvie."

Staudt stared down into the face of the young librarian, whole and uncorrupted above the blanket.

He remembered Ribbeck's question: "Why did she do it?"

Eric Staudt thought now that he had found the answer: Germany had no patent on patriotism.

2 High road to hell

THE TANK COMMANDER, Sergeant Higgins, had no idea who Deacon was or what he wanted so close to the Front. Full of zeal for the enterprise, however, the sergeant boasted that the Matilda was impervious to anti-tank shells and anything else the bloody panzers could chuck at her. She was, the sergeant went on, waxing lyrical, a spanking new model from the Vulcan works at Warrington, an A12 Mark II, with two AEC six-cylinder inline diesel engines and, while she wasn't exactly no greyhound, she had the range to carry them to St. Félice and back again without stopping to refuel.

"Ain't she a beauty, sir?"

"Absolutely," Deacon agreed and indulged the chap by patting the tank's nose plate.

The sergeant was too eager for praise to realize that he was being patronized. Deacon's smile, however charming, came nowhere near his ice-blue eyes. Deacon knew instinctively how to deal with men like Higgins, how to make sure that they not only did his bidding but respected him into the bargain. It was his one true talent. He had inherited it from his father, Sir Jeffrey St. John Deacon, 9th Baronet of Rathbone, Staffordshire, and from a string of blue-blood ancestors stretching back to 1660.

"Once we're inside and screwed up tight," said the sergeant, "we'll be safe as little 'ouses, sir."

"I'm sure we will," said Deacon. "Shall we go?"

"Right away, sir, right away."

Second Lieutenant Jeffrey Alexander Deacon had no reason to doubt the tank commander's assurances. He assumed that the geniuses in Division Four HQ, a nondescript building off the

11

Strand, would have calculated the panzers' rate of advance and matched it against the tank speed, and that a Matilda must be the most suitable form of transport for the operation. Deacon, like the tank commander, had little experience of warfare and did not understand how random its ground rules could be.

The brigade to which Deacon was formally attached had set up temporary headquarters at Manton, a couple of miles inland from the harbor at Bovet, near Dunkirk. Its business was to supply the forward battalions of the British Expeditionary Force with food, fuel and ammunition and, this past week, to prepare for evacuation. Second Lieutenant Deacon was responsible for keeping the inventory clerks up to scratch, a job that he did well but without enthusiasm. It was not what he had had in mind when he had volunteered for Special Services duty and mustered into Division Four's handpicked group of officers. He certainly hadn't damned near killed himself during twenty weeks of rigorous training in the wilds of Dorset just to spend the war with a clipboard hanging round his neck.

Patience was not Deacon's strong suit, though he saw the advantages in Division Four operatives being innocently planted in noncombatant units while awaiting allocation to specific missions.

The colonel in command of the supplies battalion and his adjutant, Captain Yatman, were aware that the raffish young subaltern was a temporary posting and that there was more to him than met the eye. As regular officers they did not quite approve of Deacon or the weird mobs that had proliferated of late, guerrilla and espionage groups whose members seemed answerable to nobody in particular.

It was with some relief, therefore, that Captain Yatman had summoned Deacon from the depot warehouse to the HQ in the St. Georges Hotel, a modest *pension* commandeered for use by the Allied forces.

Stiffly Yatman informed Deacon that he had received a coded signal from London. The transcript, on buff paper, was very long. Captain Yatman read it slowly to the Second Lieutenant who, without conscious effort, memorized the contents verbatim.

"I am instructed to ask you if you understand?" said Yatman.

"Yes, sir. I understand."

"Do you wish me to read it again?"

"No, that won't be necessary."

The captain squinted suspiciously at his subordinate.

"I still can't see what use you can possibly be in this situation, Deacon."

Deacon had been ordered to tell staff officers no more than was strictly necessary. Besides, trained or not, he had not been tested in the field and didn't want to risk Yatman's scorn if he trailed home with his tail between his legs.

"In this case, sir," Deacon said, "I assume I'm useful only because the contact, Vandeleur, can identify me on sight."

"Hm, yes," said Yatman dubiously. "I suppose with all this Fifth Column stuff flyin' about, one can't be too careful."

The captain then assured him that it would be at least three days before Guderian's tanks broke north from Abbéville and blocked the line of retreat to the boat at Boulogne. He also informed Deacon that Erwin Rommel's 7th Panzer Division had lost ground to an Allied counter-thrust at Arras which was seventy miles away and a comfortable twenty from St. Félice, the little town appointed for the rendezvous with Vandeleur.

Deacon thanked the captain for the information.

Yatman offered him the signal.

Deacon shook his head. "Has the file copy been destroyed, sir?"

"It has."

"Please destroy this one too."

"But—"

"I've got it in my head," said Deacon.

"Good God!"

The captain wished him luck, shook his hand and, while Deacon watched from the door, struck a match and held it to one corner of the signal. As soon as the last burnt crumb of paper drifted from the captain's fingers into the ashtray, Deacon turned and left the office.

He hurried to his billet, dug out his kit, packed it and hopped a ride over to the field depot at Bovet where, according to the signal, a volunteer tank crew would be put at his disposal.

Much to Deacon's surprise, crew and tank were ready and waiting.

Fifteen minutes later, at a little after midnight, Deacon squeezed himself into the tomb-like interior of the Matilda and told Sergeant Higgins to stick to the main road as far as the first map reference point at Ombreville. Diesels roared, the tank shuddered, thrust forward and crawled into the darkness that shrouded the hinterland of northern France.

It did not occur to Deacon that he could not simply cruise the thirty-eight miles to St. Félice, find Lisa Vandeleur, then toddle back to Boulogne where, apparently, a naval cutter would be waiting to whisk him across the Channel to England presumably for immediate debriefing. Deacon was unaware that the information he had received from Captain Yatman was hopelessly out of date and that in the last twenty hours the broad front of Allied resistance had narrowed to a corridor walled in by Nazi forces.

Congestion on the Rue de Bovet restricted the Matilda's progress to less than five miles per hour. Deacon, though impatient, was not unduly concerned. His rendezvous with Lisa was not scheduled to take place until noon. He was sure that the ebbing tide of military and civilian traffic would ease when they struck due east from Ombreville and that they would reach St. Félice in ample time.

Second Lieutenant Jeffrey Alexander Deacon had no way of knowing that he was already riding down the high road to hell.

An hour before daybreak the Luftwaffe's aerial bombardment of the Rue de Bovet began in earnest.

At Deacon's insistence the tank ground on through the worst of the shelling, seizing advantage of the fact that the road had miraculously cleared of foot traffic. They made eleven miles in that deafening hour, rocked but unscathed by the bombing. Beyond Ombreville, Deacon ordered the sergeant to halt the tank.

Climbing out of the turret, Deacon flagged down a passing motorcyclist, a Signals corporal who seemed anxious not to tarry. According to the corporal, who had ridden thirty miles in the last hour in spite of hazards, the panzer corps had shifted like greased lightning and now had units not far beyond the Quern canal— seven, not seventy, miles away. It was anybody's guess, said the corporal, whose side occupied St. Félice though, in his opinion, if it wasn't the Hun it soon would be.

Deacon filtered this information back to the tank commander.

"What do you think, sir? Should we turn back?" Higgins asked.

"Certainly not," Deacon retorted. "When will it be light?"

"In fifteen or twenty minutes."

"Tell you what," said Deacon, "why don't you park in the square behind the Gare Perreux—see the clock tower of the station over there—and have a brew-up? I'll walk on for a bit and see if I can find somebody who might provide accurate griff on what's happening up ahead."

"I'll send Hopkins with you."

"No need. Let the lads enjoy their tea. I'm not going far."

"It's bloody quiet out there. Too bloody quiet for my likin'."

"Frankly, I'm rather concerned that the bombers have destroyed the canal bridge. If the bridge is impassable we'll have to detour twelve miles south-west to find another large enough to support a tank."

"But we haven't fuel for—"

"Quite!" said Deacon curtly.

The lieutenant clambered from the turret and climbed down to the cobbles. He had a Webley revolver, field-glasses and map with him but left the rest of his kit behind. He leaned against the breast of the tank for a moment to take his bearings.

The sergeant called, "Know your way about 'ere, sir?"

"Yes, I've been here before," Deacon answered and set off down the narrow avenue that would bring him to the *quai* and the Café d'Or.

Now that the light had strengthened he could readily identify landmarks, little shops under tiled eaves, fourteenth-century buildings carefully preserved. There was some damage, pock-marks of shrapnel on walls, tiles and glass lying on the cobbles, but considerably less than he had expected.

With the bombers gone and shelling ceased, the silence in the town was uncanny. The click of Deacon's heels seemed as loud as castanets. A backyard rooster crowed and small birds chittered in blossom trees behind the houses. A ginger tomcat licked itself on a high wall and flocks of pigeons poised along the gutters like tiny caped hangmen. But there were no lamps in any windows, no signs of human habitation. It was as if a plague had rampaged through Quern.

Quite alone, Deacon walked on, revolver cocked, nerves taut, blue eyes alert.

It was four years, give or take a summer, since he had last strolled the streets of Quern. Fatigued by his final term at Oxford, he had sneaked off in the Allard for a motoring trip across the Continent. He had intended to spend only one night in the Artois but then he had met the girl, and the girl had attracted him and he had suddenly realized what he had been missing during those final monastic months of study, what he needed to revive his flagging spirits.

The seduction had been swift. At twenty Deacon had had more than his share of women. Sexual precocity was another family trait, the pursuit of girls a dominant family interest. But he had behaved well with Lisa, and she had been willing. It helped that he spoke the language. She was on holiday too, staying with a cousin on a farm in the neighborhood. She had taught him much that he did not know about the bloody history of Flanders and Picardy. Most of that had drifted out of his memory. What he remembered were the long warm afternoons and, in particular, their love-making.

Deacon had left Quern, at the end of a fortnight, imagining that he would never see Lisa again. It had startled him when her name had been read out by Yatman. He could not envisage the girl to whom he had made love in the Hotel Vallière as an active partisan. For all that, even in the extraordinary circumstances of war, he looked forward to seeing her again.

The lieutenant reached the mouth of the avenue where the whitewashed house of the blacksmith stood. It too was boarded and abandoned. When he turned the corner and looked expectantly down to the corner of the Quai de Emil Ducasse he found that the Café d'Or had gone. Nothing remained of it but an ugly ruin. It seemed quite ancient for there was no smoke, and the debris was plastered with pale dust, like flour. Deacon felt angry, then wistful. He was no student now, no conquering lover. He was a soldier in an alien uniform and had not come here out of choice.

Dogs scavenged among the mounds but there were no other signs of life. Even the grizzled old women who had gossiped at the bench by the water trough had been whisked away; to the young Jeffrey Deacon they had seemed as immovable as marble monuments. Apparently the good folk of Quern had succumbed to panic and had fled out into the fields to hide from the war.

Hands on his hips, fingers curled about the revolver, Deacon scanned the watercourse. Across the canal bomb damage was even less extensive though the sky behind him, over the roof of the Gare Perreux, was hung with ropes of smoke.

Suddenly Deacon stopped thinking about the girl.

The Stukas came out of the smoke, flying low and fast. Three, four, six of them fanned out and staggered in bombing formation. Deacon could not imagine why they would want to bomb a deserted square at the back of the Gare Perreux. For a moment he had forgotten about the tank. The Matilda was a sitting duck. A high snarling whine preceded the planes, predicting the bomb sticks that would dart down, dark against the pearl-gray sky of dawn.

Deacon dived for the slot in the side of an upright iron *pissoir* that had escaped damage in the night bombardment. He cowered against its rusted metal wall, arms wrapped over his head. He had left his steel helmet back in the tank, and his respirator. God, what if the Stukas were dropping gas bombs? Deacon began to shake. At this precise moment Jeff Deacon realized how little he really knew about war. One vital factor had not been taken into account in all the training lectures he had attended. Confusion. Not only was he confused, everybody seemed to be confused, the Stuka pilots included. Disgorging thirty or forty bombs into the empty heart of a tiny provincial town was just plain crazy. Deacon could only surmise that they had overshot their prescribed targets, the ant-like columns of soldiers and civilians retreating to the Channel ports, perhaps, or some stubborn pocket of resistance along the flanks of the canal. But if the panzer divisions *were* streaking in pursuit of the BEF was it likely that the Luftwaffe had been briefed to destroy the only big bridge for miles around?

God knows! Perhaps fat Hermann Goering was as crazy as Adolf.

Perhaps they were all crazy.

Crazy, crazy, crazy.

Mad. Mad. Mad.

All—bloody—mad.

The words exploded in Deacon's mind as the bombs went off. The *pissoir* rocked on its concrete piles. Its metallic walls rang with a rain of shrapnel.

Suddenly Deacon was absolutely certain that the six German divebombers had been briefed to get his Matilda. He gave a stifled cry of rage and resentment while the Stukas climbed away on screaming trails, leaving echoes of the bomb-blasts in their wake and a slow profound growling rumble, like a flood in the town's drains. Curled against the inner wall of the snail-shaped *pissoir*, Deacon did not move. Between his knees he could see a section of stained iron and stone coping. He watched it quiver and tremble and, against a slant of thin sunlight which angled under the shell, saw a fine sifting dust settle on his boots and cling to the nap of his trousers, marking him, like flour, as it had marked the debris of the Café d'Or.

"Bastards," he said softly.

He scrambled to his feet and went out of the *pissoir* and glanced back at the Gare Perreux and saw that its handsome clock-tower was gone, and knew from the smoke and raddled skyline what had taken the hit. He ran back the way he had come, up the narrow cobbled streets to the square by the railway station. The damage became more apparent the closer the lieutenant came to the Gare Perreux where blast and flying shrapnel had broken windows and brought down walls. When he rounded into the square he knew at once that his premonition had been absolutely correct.

The west-facing gable of the station had been stove in, the ornate clock-tower demolished. A tangle of telegraph wires writhed across the cobbles and a row of closet-like shops almost totally destroyed. The ticket office had been struck too and reels of pink *cartes* and white dockets were blowing gently across the mouth of the Rue Tibulle, fanned by warm air from burning woodwork and the long red ragged spill of flame from the Matilda's gas tank.

Skirting the trail of burning fuel, Deacon walked stiffly towards the listing hulk of the tank. Through the smoke, like phantoms, he glimpsed six or eight townspeople scurrying silently away into the shadows of the Rue Tibulle, like peasants evading the bony hand of death in a Breughel painting. They were old, he supposed, and bemused and too scared to try to aid the Englishmen who had come into their town, equating them, perhaps, with the Stukas which flung havoc from the air. Deacon did not even call out to them and they were gone behind the crackling flames before it occurred to him that he could have used their help.

Mercifully the young lieutenant did not have to enter the hulk of the tank to find out what he had to know. Two bombs, he guessed, had finished it. Perhaps only one. The sergeant was draped from the turret, head down, shoulders wisping black smoke. He did not look like anyone that Deacon had ever known before. Deacon walked round the wrecked Matilda in a cautious semi-circle until he found the driver and gunner, who had obviously been out of the tank at the time of the surprise air attack. Brewing tea? Of course! The can of drinking water was intact, standing upright where the gunner had laid it when he had started for cover. Gunner Hopkins had been shot cleanly in the back and lay on his belly with his legs stretched perfectly straight and his hands and arms extended above his head, like a diver caught in the act of plunging into a pool.

Deacon had an urge to sneak away like the French peasants, to avoid the acts that he must perform as an officer and gentleman.

He went to the body and stooped.

Blood had burst out through the gunner's chest. His belly was a soft raspberry mush. Deacon turned his head away, hesitated, decided it was pointless to feel for a heartbeat, checked the pulse in the wrist and found no flicker of life. It was stupid to expect it, really. He was relieved. He had no notion what he would have done if the man had been not dead but dying. How would he have coped with that? It was another of the things he hadn't been taught in training camp. He got up and moved on, walking on his toes as if afraid that he might disturb the corpses.

The driver was a very young man, with a round head and gangling limbs. He had spoken, Deacon recalled, with a cheerful Lancastrian accent, like George Formby. He had not, it appeared, been wearing his tin helmet. He would have been severely reprimanded by his CSM if he had been caught without it while on duty. The helmet, however, wouldn't have saved him. The driver had been very close to the blast. He had been lifted and flung through the window of an abandoned shop, his uniform shredded by glass and shrapnel. When Deacon gingerly reached into the broken shop-front and, with finger and thumb, groped for the pulse on the hanging left arm, the body slumped. Deacon saw that the boy's face had been wiped away, leaving only a bloody sponge freckled with gristle and shards of bone.

Deacon dropped the arm, pivoted and vomited discreetly against the shop wall. There wasn't much to come. He hadn't eaten in ten hours.

When it was over, Deacon wiped his mouth and chin with an issue handkerchief, balled the cotton and tossed it away. He did not look back at the corpse displayed in the shattered recess of the window.

Instead, shoulders squared and spine straight, Second Lieutenant Deacon set off towards the canal again, heading for the Quern bridge and St. Félice.

When the spotter plane droned overhead, a flimsy little gnat of a thing, Deacon did not break stride. The swastika on the plane's tail fin was vivid and ugly. The plane ignored him and droned over the rooftops, out of sight.

Deacon stopped and scowled up at the sky. Rage broke loose like floodwater.

He shook his fist at the empty sky.

"Bastards," he shouted. "Murdering bastards."

Then he hurried on towards the canal, sick and furious at having come unstuck only seventeen inland miles from the coast.

Sergeant Buz Campbell, the Royal Langhams' self-appointed demolitions expert, and his sidekick, Corporal P. B. McNair, were cooking breakfast. The mess tin was planted on bricks set round a wood fire and its contents smelled delicious. When the Stukas made their run over the town, Campbell quickly covered the pan with a steel helmet. But the explosions were a half-mile to the south and dust didn't endanger the gravy.

In the pan were choice cuts from the carcasses of two flop-eared rabbits that P.B. had rescued from a hutch in back of a cottage on the far side of the canal. P.B. had neatly broken the bunnies' necks and carried them back to Buz by the ears, one in each hand. He had grinned his mute demonic grin and nodded while the sergeant had slagged him by way of praise for his enterprise. But the big Canadian had other things to think of just then and the rabbits had had to wait while he had gotten on with the job of wiring the bridge.

The Quern bridge was a single trestle fixed structure set high above the canal on two old but solid timber crib piers. In the very last of the light Buz had stripped off, slipped into the black water and swum slowly around the piers. Rebuilt after the last war, the timbers were dogged and spiked, the points of intersection beautifully adzed. He had already walked across the bridge looking in vain for a classification sign. He figured the span would fall into military class 18, which meant it could support the PzKpfw Mark II light tanks that the panzer corps' front runners were using and, later, would give clearway to medium artillery and all kinds of trucks—if it was left standing.

If it had been up to goddamned Captain Trevor Whiteside, the remnants of the platoon would have galloped over the bridge and straight on through the town, with never a thought for delaying the enemy on their heels. Captain Trevor Whiteside had inherited the command only that morning when his OC had been shot in the throat by a sniper. Consequently Captain Whiteside was shit-scared and not thinking straight.

Supposedly Whiteside was answering a call from the shake-down of what was left of the 3rd and 5th Divisions to rendezvous at some monument on the Rue de Cassel seven miles west of Quern and to retreat "in orderly fashion" from there to Dunkirk to prepare for a full-scale evacuation. But Campbell figured it would come to a showdown long before they sniffed the sea. For the last twenty miles of the retreat he had been gathering items he thought he might need, picking them from ditches and fields, squirreling them away under the tarp on their one support truck until the acting QM howled that there was no more room since the truck was also carrying wounded and rations. After that Campbell carried the gear on his back, with P.B.'s help, of course. When he clapped eyes on the bridge at the canal at Quern, Buz Campbell knew he had found the perfect place to make a stand.

"What do you say, P.B.?"

P.B. had shrugged, thinking it might be no bad idea to shake off the platoon since then they would have the leisure to cook the bunnies properly and not have to share. Anyhow, the little town looked deserted and there was enough of it still standing, most of it in fact, so he figured they would be able to loot enough booze to keep him pissed for the rest of the fuckin' war. Then too, P.B. was also sick of dragging his ass away from the krauts, smarting at what had been done to the division at Bonneteur with three hundred dead or wounded and twice that number taken prisoner.

"Anyhow," Buz Campbell muttered, "what's gonna happen when we reach the beach? Magic fuckin' carpets? If the krauts don't nail us here, they'll nail us there. Right, wee man?"

P.B. had nodded stoically.

"Captain Whiteside, sir. It's my opinion we could gain a valuable amount of time if somebody stayed behind to destroy this bridge," Buz had suggested.

"The section is so quiet, so *abominably* quiet."

"The bridge, Captain Whiteside?"

"What? What's that you say, Campbell?"

Patiently Campbell had explained what he had in mind.

"Can't understand why it hasn't been done," the captain complained. "Where are the Sappers? Where are the RAF?"

"Somewheres else, sir."

Whiteside had pulled himself together long enough to take stock of the situation.

Campbell was sympathetic. He could understand why the officer was unnerved. They had been through nine hellish days, fighting and retreating, fighting again, left without proper transport to get themselves back to the battalion. And without clear orders. Whiteside was one of those guys who desperately needed orders. Besides, the last eight miles into Quern had been nerve-tinglers of a different kind. The hamlets and villages were like graveyards, the silence and lack of bustle uncanny. There were few signs of fighting and not much destruction, yet the population had vanished. Campbell figured the main roads to the north and south had attracted the traffic like magnetic bars. There had been a few long-boats on the canal, puttering along, but they had vanished too with the coming of dusk.

Whiteside had finally realized what the bluff Canadian sergeant was driving at. "Oh, you mean bring down the bridge to delay the German tanks?"

"Yeah, that's what I mean, sir."

"But—explosives? We don't have any explosives in the lorry, do we?"

"We do, sir."

Whiteside didn't ask how or why. Perhaps the captain had forgotten that they were an infantry company, or the remnants of one. He didn't even remark on the French Hotchkiss machine gun that Campbell had slung over his shoulders, in addition to his full field kit and issue rifle. P.B. toted two full ammo chests, one under each arm.

"But—but—do you know what to do with explosives?" said Whiteside. "I wouldn't want to be responsible for—for bungling, you understand."

"I've used dynamite before, sir, when I was a logger, home in Canada."

"I see. What do you suggest?"

"Corporal McNair and me, we'll wait behind. I'll wire and blow the bridge just as soon as I'm sure none of our troops are still trapped in the sector."

"Wait for the Germans, do you mean?"

Buz Campbell was tempted to tell the captain the truth, tell him he would wait until he could see the whites of their eyes and the fillings in their fuckin' teeth. But he was an old sweat, a regular soldier, and had learned how to handle guys like Whiteside.

"It'll give you time to get clear, sir. The krauts won't move on without their tanks. They haven't got infantry support up this far, yet. Can't have, captain. After we engaged them at Bonneteur they pulled back. Remember? The infantry, the German infantry?"

"My orders, such as they are, are to retreat with all possible haste and without further engagement of the enemy, to—"

"Initiative, sir," Campbell had said softly.

"What? Lord, yes!"

Maybe the bewildered and harrassed officer would have argued some more but a squadron of strafing fighters had come winging in from the flank at that instant and scattered the column into the cottage gardens that bordered the road to the bridge.

Campbell lay in sappy grass with one arm around the captain's shoulder.

"See, they're tryin' to drive us back, sir," he said. "They guess we're gonna try to blow it and they don't want us to."

Campbell had other ideas. The Stukas were strays. The advancing panzers were not close, at least not on a direct line down the side road that came into Quern across the diagonal of the canal. He kept the opinion to himself.

"What do you say, captain?"

"Can you—can you do it?"

"Sure."

"How—how many men will you need?"

"Me and Corporal McNair can handle it."

"All right, all right, sergeant. You have my permission."

When the planes had gone the captain mustered the hundred and eleven remaining soldiers, led by their one heavy lorry, and hastened away across the bridge and up the main street of the town of Quern into the lavender dusk, leaving Sergeant Buz Campbell, Corporal P. B. McNair and a pile of looted equipment behind on the west bank of the canal.

"Thank Christ for that," Buz Campbell sighed.

If P.B. thought he was in for a night's boozing, however, Buz soon disillusioned him. The sergeant kept his Scots buddy, his pocket beetle, at work far into the night. Even so, P.B. did manage to slip off long enough to scare up two bottles of Hollands gin and six bottles of red wine. Campbell was glad of the gin when he finally hauled himself from the cold waters of the Quern canal. He had sunk explosives in the west bank pier, digging fork detonators into the sticky sweet-smelling stuff and trailing cable back to the charge box.

Wrapped in a blanket and a quilt that P.B. had found, the sergeant had rested for half an hour before clambering under the bridge to plant the remaining explosives in the cross braces. It was 3 a.m. before he returned to the foxhole P.B. had built in a shelled cottage in a tiny green garden close to the top of the ramp. P.B. had used old planks and pieces of an iron stove to construct a barricade and had bedded the firing position with the eiderdown and blankets. He had set up the Hotchkiss, the Bren and the rifles and had put the detonator box, unprimed, close at hand. He had also finished most of one bottle of Hollands.

Campbell let P.B. sleep while he kept watch for the armies of the Reich. P.B. didn't even stir when the hour-long aerial bombardment shook the town. Maybe nights had been noisier in the brawling Glasglow tenement where P.B. had been born and raised.

Buz Campbell, however, was wide awake. He knew what they would be up against. He had smelt powder before. Like P.B., he was a soldier by choice, not a conscript. Back in 1934—twenty-seven years old and sick of bumming around—he had come to Britain from Canada to join the Royal Langham Rifles. His old man had served with the outfit in the last great war and Buz had been weaned on tales of fighting men. Now that he had walked the battlefields and through the war graves, he figured he would have been better staying home in Vancouver or up in the high country of the Slocan Valley, leaving the old man with dreams of a glory that never was. Perhaps it was the nature of warfare that had changed, Campbell thought. Perhaps it was no longer a brave stubborn game but something swift, lethal and evil.

As soon as it was light, the Canadian skinned and cut up the rabbits, lit a fire in the camp hearth and got on with cooking. The sun was up and warm, the sector peaceful, when sergeant and corporal sat down to breakfast.

They ate straight from the mess tin with fingers and spoons. The meat was flaky and sweet, fresh spring vegetables stewed soft in a gravy of red wine and condensed milk.

"How is it, wee man?" Campbell asked.

P.B. grunted, rolled his eyes and thrust a hot gobbet of meat into his mouth.

They drank wine from the bottle. Buz let P.B. have his fill. He figured from the sounds that carried on the warm misty morning air that the tanks would not arrive before noon at the earliest.

P.B. still hadn't asked him why they hadn't blown the bridge and cleared out after their comrades. P.B. was smart. He guessed what was in Buz's mind. He didn't have to have it spelled out for him.

P.B. knew they were waiting for the krauts to show up.

Merely demolishing a bridge wasn't enough for Sergeant Campbell. He reckoned to blow it when it was weighted with tanks, to wreak a little hell before they lit out. If the Germans spotted the charges, he could blast the thing under their noses, no harm done. Admittedly he would have felt more secure if P.B. had managed to find some kind of transport but there wasn't so much as a fuckin' roller-skate left in the town. What the hell! Three hundred Langhams had died this week already. Couple more wouldn't make much difference.

Campbell supped gravy and studied the gun-metal strip of water and the gut of the country road where it kinked out of the trees and broadened on to the ramp.

"You," said the voice. "I say, what do you think you're up to?"

Buz flung the pan one way and rolled the other. He grabbed for the Bren gun and rolled again, came up in a sitting position close against the stove-pipe barricade, ready to fire. P.B. had vanished like a shadow. Buz had seen the pocket beetle in action before. The little Scots diehard would have the intruder in the sights of his Lee Enfield, finger twitching on the trigger.

The stranger stood in full view thirty yards below the emplacement on the step that led down to the canal. How he had got there without being spotted was more than Buz could imagine. He didn't look like a slinker, though he must have moved like one, coming quiet and sly from the flank, to beat their eyes and ears. He showed himself now, though—hands raised, palms open, head held back in an arrogant English-officer manner that no kraut could emulate. He was blond, lean, handsome and his pips said he was a lieutenant.

"British, British, for God's sake." It was half babble, half command. "I'm a British officer."

"Hold it, wee man," Buz Campbell shouted.

Campbell got to his knees and peered over the wall. Not another living soul in sight.

"Come forward, sir." The sergeant still couldn't pick out P.B., his ace in the hole in case this was some new trick the krauts had gotten up to.

The lieutenant's uniform was flecked with dust. He carried no kit, not even a respirator, only binoculars and a holstered sidearm.

"Can you identify yourself, sir?" asked Campbell.

"My name is Deacon. I'm an officer with the supplies unit of the Fourth Battalion of the Armored," said the lieutenant, peevishly. "Who the devil are you?"

"Langhams."

Campbell caught sight of P.B., way down below the steps by the arm of the lock, a hundred yards from the bridge end.

"Hey, wee man," he cried, "is this guy alone?"

P.B. waved. All Clear.

"I understand your reluctance to take me on trust." The lieutenant came cautiously forward. "But I give you my word that I'm alone."

"How did you get here?"

"By tank."

"A tank?" Campbell perked up. He sure could use a tank about now. "Where is it?"

"In the square of the station. Wrecked," said the lieutenant. "The crew are dead."

"How did you escape—sir?"

"I was on recce," said the lieutenant. "The Stukas—you must have seen them—unloaded their bombs into the square. By the look of it our Matilda took a direct hit."

"Can she be salvaged?"

"I doubt it."

"She wasn't toting any special arms; an anti-tank gun, maybe?"

"I'm afraid not."

"One last question, sir," said Campbell. "What's a supplies officer doing in a Matilda in this godforsaken hole?"

"I was on my way to the Front."

Campbell laughed. "Hell, you don't need a tank for that. Stick around and the Front'll come to you, sir."

"May I put my hands down now?"

"Sure, come on in." Campbell gestured with the muzzle of the Bren and ushered the lieutenant into the emplacement.

"All the comforts of home, I see," said the lieutenant. "Where are the rest of your lot?"

"Moved on. There's just me and him." P.B. entered the rear of the ruined cottage, grinning, the Lee Enfield held ready. "We—uh—we got stranded, sir, when the rest of the boys were called back."

"Stranded," said the lieutenant. It wasn't, Campbell reckoned, a question. "I see. Stranded in a convenient position overlooking the Quern canal bridge."

"Hey, is that what it's called?" Campbell laid down the Bren gun and lifted an uncorked bottle of wine. "Care to wet your tubes, lieutenant?"

"Absolutely." The lieutenant took the bottle and sucked from it.

He had one of those prominent, bobbing Adam's apples, Campbell noticed, the kind you find on rednecks and members of the English upper crust.

The lieutenant handed back the empty bottle. "Sorry. I seem to have scoffed it all. I was rather dry, I'm afraid."

"Plenty in stock, sir," said Campbell.

"You wouldn't have anything to eat, by any chance?"

"Some pretty gritty rabbit."

"That'll do."

Buz retrieved the remains of the rabbit stew from the corner of the fox-hole and washed the pieces of meat with wine. He placed them in the mess tin and passed it over to the stranger, who ate hungrily but fastidiously.

"You know," the lieutenant said, "I've never seen dead men before. At least, not men who died in that manner. Violently."

He glanced at the piece of meat in his fingers, paused, shrugged and pushed it into his mouth.

"All things considered," he said, "I suppose it was quick and merciful."

"Never knew what hit them," said Buz. He figured the lieutenant to be a novice, haunted by the Matilda's blood-wetted coffin and its three dismembered corpses, but the ice-blue eyes gave nothing away.

The lieutenant went on eating.

Crouched on his haunches, P.B. watched the officer intently

while Buz unearthed a second bottle of Hollands from his sack and drew the cork with his teeth.

"Try some of this, sir."

The lieutenant did not appear to hear him.

"How far off are the Germans, do you suppose?" he asked.

"Can't say," Buz answered. "Might be six miles, might be ten."

"Have they captured St. Félice, do you know?"

"We didn't come through St. Félice. We held at Bailleul yesterday. Pulled back in the early afternoon."

"Bailleul is to the west, isn't it?"

"I guess it is. What's on your mind, lieutenant?"

"I'd like to reach St. Félice."

"Well, I figure there's a hundred thousand BEF soldiers in there, but where and in what strengths only God knows."

"It's only eight miles down that road."

"That road?" said Buz politely. "You wanna go down *that* road?"

"My orders are to reach St. Félice," said Deacon.

P.B. chuckled and settled his back against the wall. Though used to daft laddies in officers' uniforms he found them unfailingly amusing.

"If you blow up the bridge," said Deacon, "I'm not going to be able to ride back, am I?"

It was all Buz Campbell could do to keep a straight face. He did not dare glance at the pocket beetle or he could have burst out laughing. P.B.'s expression would be blank, except for the dark eyes which would have the glitter of suppressed laughter in them, a withering scorn that was the Scot's response to all things that he did not understand.

"Yeah, I figure you'd be able to ride back, sir," said Buz.

"Oh, really?"

"Sure, if the panzer divisions arrive here intact—and it don't look to me like there's much out there to stop 'em—then their sappers'll have a bridge up in a couple of hours. I don't mean no string. I mean a pontoon strong enough to take armor."

"They're that efficient, are they?"

"Goddamned right, sir."

"What's the cover like?"

"Flattish. Some trees, and a wooded ridge to the left. Farms."

"Still inhabited?"

"I guess so," said Buz. "Look, what's so important about reaching St. Félice?"

"I've been ordered to rendezvous with a French national there." P.B. made a noise like a snore.

"I realize your corporal finds it all very risible," said Deacon, "but I assure you it's no joke. I must reach St. Félice as soon as possible."

"Even if it's in German hands?"

"Yes."

"You're a cert to be taken prisoner," said Buz.

"Not necessarily."

"Are you asking us to hold the canal bridge?" said Buz.

"I'm asking you to accompany me."

"Yeah, I thought that was it," said Buz Campbell.

"Even if the town has fallen," said Deacon, "I'm sure we can make our way there under cover of darkness."

"Well, it's pretty goddamned chaotic out there. But the Germans have one up on us," Buz said. "They're on the attack. They're travellin' hell for leather to cut off the BEF retreat to the coast."

"In that case, where are they?"

"I reckon they're being mustered at a fresh start point," said the sergeant. "Maybe they've run out of gas or gotten ahead of the infantry. I don't know. But one thing I do know, something big and heavy is gonna come up that road sooner or later, and I don't want to walk smack into it."

"I see," said Deacon. "That's why the shelling and bombing have stopped. The Germans are keeping the Quern road clear for an advance of heavy tanks?"

"Could be." Buz Campbell glanced at his wristwatch. "It's eighteen hours since we last sighted a kraut. They've been swarming forward for eleven days. Now, suddenly, they've stopped."

"But *where* have they stopped?" said the lieutenant. "That's the rub, isn't it?"

He drank another mouthful of gin neat from the bottle. He dabbed his lips with his sleeve, took a silver cigarette case from his tunic pocket, opened it and offered it to Campbell.

"French Caporals, I'm afraid," Deacon apologized.

Campbell took one of the cigarettes. He gestured to P.B. who crabbed over and waited expectantly at the officer's elbow.

"Okay if he has one too, sir?" said Buz.

"By all means."

Deacon swivelled the open case and the corporal helped himself to one of the fat, loose-packed French smokes. The lieutenant's lighter was as fancy as his case. Buz noticed how P.B.'s eyes followed the items speculatively as Deacon returned them to his pocket.

For fully a minute the three smoked in silence. From the north came the distinct papping chatter of machine-gun fire, punctuated by sporadic barks from anti-tank guns. Dust from columns moving on the main roads towards St. Omer, stained the sky with a brownish haze.

"If we had the right sort of transport," said Campbell suddenly, "I could have us to St. Félice and back again in a couple of hours."

"Have you had a look around?"

"Can't find no wheels at all." Campbell shrugged.

"If we walked in the direction of St. Félice, what are our chances of picking up a ride?"

Buz ignored the question. "What's to come out, sir?" he said. "What are you so all-fired anxious to save from the krauts?"

"A person."

"Why couldn't they make it out under their own steam?"

"I don't know," said Deacon. "I wasn't told."

"Who is this person?"

"I haven't a clue," said Deacon. "But as my mob sent me in from the coast in a tank, it occurs to me that the person I have to collect is only moderately important. In other words, it was decided to risk no more than a second lieutenant and one tank."

"You figure they don't expect you to come back?"

"If that's the case," said Deacon, "it will give me great pleasure to prove them wrong."

"I guess you wouldn't want to tell me who issued the order?"

"I guess," said Deacon with a smile, "I wouldn't."

"Looks like we'll just have to take you on trust, sir."

"I appreciate it, sergeant."

"All right with you, wee man?" Buz Campbell inquired.

"Aye, right," P.B. answered.

Deacon pushed himself to his feet and ground out the cigarette butt beneath his heel.

"Now all we have to do is find suitable transport," he said.

P.B. gripped the young lieutenant's wrist and drew him down again. Sergeant, corporal and officer, on their knees, peered over the stove-pipe barricade as the lead rider of a group of six tooled his motorcycle sidecar into sight and slewed to a halt at the far end of the bridge.

"Something like that, lieutenant?" Buz Campbell inquired.

"Why, yes, indeed," said Jeff Deacon. "Something like that would do very nicely."

"How many do you count, P.B.?"

"Six."

"Reconnaissance scouts," said Campbell. "Riding ahead of the heavy mob."

"How far ahead?"

"Could be as much as ten miles."

"They aren't ordinary panzers, are they?" said Deacon.

"Christ, no!" the sergeant answered. "They're SS."

"How in God's name," said Deacon, "do we persuade a dozen armed SS troops to hand over their motorcycles?"

"Leave that to me, sir," Buz Campbell said.

Peter Bennet McNair had an infallible instinct for terrain. He had developed the noble art as a wee laddie in Glasgow's Gorbals, in its loans and backcourt middens and later in pubs and betting shops. The reason he bore no scars, or a police record as long as a tallyman's reach, was because he had learned how to hit and run.

The McNairs were born fighters. P.B. had fought with his brothers for the dregs of the beer his Ma left, for the scrap ends of meat and shrivelled sausages after his Pa had his fill, had fought over card games and pitch-and-toss and the relative merits of

Scottish football-teams and boxers. He had fought with his sisters too, gaunt bitches, worse than the boys, rolling on the floor with them, flapping a hand in front of his face to keep their nails from his eyes, hauling at their hair, until he learned how he could stop them by groping them right between the legs, which would make them recoil long enough for him to wriggle out of their clutches. He couldn't quite remember why he fought with his sisters, except that they were prone to fly off the handle and it was, in a funny way, exciting to wrestle with girls.

By the time P.B. was fourteen he had had ten years training in guerrilla warfare. Small though he was, he had already acquired a reputation which brought him to the attention of Solly Mahafee, a Scots Irish Jew who owned half the tenement properties and all the rackets between Commercial Road and Bridge Street. P.B. had worked for Solly Mahafee for four years before moving over the river to join big Harry Lorne who had loan company interests to protect. P.B. was doing all right until the night when a drunken gambler called Minto, who fancied himself a hard man, pulled a chisel on him. Minto had got himself stabbed for his stupidity. For four days Minto lay on death's doorstep in the Western Infirmary. Only the skill of surgeons finally pulled him through. Solly—not Lorne—gave P.B. some fatherly advice and told him to clear out of Scotland. Before the week was out, the Royal Langhams had a new recruit.

Against all the odds, P.B. took to army life. Soon he didn't give a shit about the Gorbals or Glasgow gangs. He was shrewd enough to toe the military line in exchange for three squares a day, six shillings week to squander on cigarettes and beer, and a rifle of his own. Two years and one month after Private McNair completed basic training, Great Britain declared war on Adolf Hitler and P.B. found an enemy worthy of his mettle. He also found a boss who was more demanding than Solly and Harry Lorne rolled into a lump, by which P.B. didn't mean the British Army but his big Canadian pal, Sergeant Buz Campbell.

Buz quickly became P.B.'s idol. Buz was the only man P.B. had ever met whom he felt he could trust right down to the wire. For starters, Buz was twice P.B.'s size and seemed to know a lot about everything, having travelled to places P.B. had never even heard of and done things P.B. had only seen done in Hollywood pictures. P.B. respected Sergeant Campbell. In a funny sort of way, he was respected in return in spite of the fact that the Sarge constantly gave him the rough edge of his tongue.

That particular May morning in the town of Quern, P.B. didn't have to listen very hard to comprehend the sergeant's plan of action. He had already worked it out for himself. The lieutenant would remain in the fox-hole to give covering fire when the balloon went up. P.B. would have preferred to have a ranker handling the Hotchkiss because most officers were nancies when it came to guns. P.B. would be sure to keep a weather eye behind him for there was more than one British private lying dead out there with a British bullet accidentally buried in his spine. Somebody had to do it, though, and it was better than having the lieutenant running loose. Anyhow the lieutenant claimed he could cope with the gun and Buz took his word for it. Maybe this particular nance would turn out okay.

While Buz whispered instructions, P.B. rid himself of the clutter of webbing that regulations obliged him to tote about. He even took off his heavy serge battledress blouse, packing what he would need into the commodious pockets of his trousers. He slipped extra ammo into the large patch pocket on his thigh where he could feel its weight.

"Jesus, wee man, you're not going on a goddamned picnic," Buz Campbell said. "At least wear your tin lid."

Obediently P.B. tapped the helmet on to his head and tightened the strap so that it bit into the stubble under his chin.

"How much ammo do you have?"

"Sixty rounds, Buz."

"Should do."

"No grenades?" the lieutenant asked.

" 'Fraid not, sir," said Buz.

"What about the Bren?"

"It's a rifle job," said Buz. "We mustn't damage the motor-cycles. We need at least two of them intact."

Standing behind the serrated brick at the front of the cottage, Buz spied out the lie of the land.

"Right, wee man?"

"Aye."

"Then go."

P.B. went.

He carried his Lee Enfield in one hand, trailing it. It might have been part of him. The ammo clips clicked slightly in his pocket. He put his right hand across the thigh pocket to keep the metal quiet and ran on, stooped.

Head and shoulders thrust forward, the corporal dodged through bushes, through a wicket gate at the rear of the cottage, vaulted a low stone wall, veered left along the back of a shed and hopped over another low wall on to a narrow strip of waste ground. Garden rubbish had been dumped here and tall weeds and blackthorn bushes flourished. He traversed the dump to the crest of a grass bank, no more than three feet high, below which were the ramp and half-paved sweep of the bridge road.

P.B. crouched there, not even breathing hard.

Through hanging thorn blossoms he could make out the cottage gable, gaudy yellow brick and squiggles of ivy. He was looking into the sun now and didn't wait around in case of glitter. He shot right again, bent double, rump up. He could smell the hot aromatic odors of dew-dampened earth and weeds, then he was out on to the road, going diagonally up towards the town. He travelled fast, following much the same route he had taken when the lieutenant had surprised them a half-hour ago. A couple of minutes later he reached the second of the two canal cottages, this one on the south side of the Quern road. The building was more or less intact. He scuttled past its gable wall and across a trimmed lawn about the size of a postcard and through a blue-painted gate in a privet hedge which brought him out not ten yards from the huge oaken arm of a lock gate, chained in an open position.

Seconds later P.B. was safely stationed behind the lock arm, protected by a couple of big iron bollards sunk into the concrete. He had a perfect view of the bridge, both banks. Range on the Quern end of the bridge was under two hundred yards, more like one-sixty, easy meat for a punter who could group ten shots into a two-inch circle at four hundred yards, twice the testing requirement for a Lee Enfield combat rifle. P.B. placed the rifle across his thighs and, sitting on his heels, arranged seven magazines in a neat line on the flagstone close at hand. Seven ten-round magazines:

P.B. could fire the bolt-action weapon at thirty aimed rounds per minute, faster if he was really souped up. Quietly the corporal laid the Lee Enfield's muzzle across the convex upper surface of the lock arm. He tipped back his helmet and settled to mark the quarry.

The motorcyclists remained clustered on the far side of the canal. None of the drivers had dismounted and all the sidecar soldiers were seated in their boxes. They were arguing among themselves. P.B. could hear the guttural jabber and grinned at their queer jerky gestures. Buz had said he should look for a mounted wireless set but he could not see one, though the bikes were bunched so close, engines revving, that he couldn't see much at all. He sighted through the rifle's aperture. He felt very sharp this morning, with meat in his belly and a good night's kip behind him and no snotty-nosed officer bitching at him to keep his head down and his chin up.

Impatient for the action to begin, P.B. waited, chest resting against the big smooth wooden spar. He could smell the canal. It smelled like all canals, dirty and metallic, not like rivers which smelled like lentil broth. He laid his hands out in the sun. They were smooth and brown and as steady as the oak on which they rested.

Cheerfully, soundlessly, P.B. whistled "I Belong to Glasgow."

Then they were coming—sudden and swift—expertly swirling the bikes out of the huddle in a spray of dust, engines roaring, soldiers in the cars swaying, uncoiling into a column, out on to the bridge, six machines swooping across the span.

P.B. saw a big-winged bird rise up from the surface of the water and skim away under the bridge, heading out of trouble. Lazily the corporal slid his finger into the guard, laid the ball against the trigger and lifted the bolt from its lugs with his left thumb.

The lead cyclist bounced out on to the ramp.

"C'mon, c'mon," P.B. said softly.

The bridge disintegrated. Span and piles went one after the other. The road across the trestles dipped and slipped down, while fragments of the structure hurled into the sky. The pier wallowed into the water, hauling the road with it into the canal.

The krauts never knew what hit them.

The third combo plunged straight into the crumbling wall of

wood blocks. P.B. saw the driver somersault over the handlebars into the water. The machine was completely engulfed, the engine sound swallowed up by thunderous explosions. Shocked air wafted past P.B.'s face. The first pattering debris sprinkled the flagstones around him. He didn't flinch, didn't blink, didn't even look at the havoc on the bridge any more. He was only vaguely aware of bodies and motorbikes sailing off in all directions.

So far, it was a great wee plan.

The two combos which had cleared the bridge slewed on to the open half-acre of ramp and road. There were no krauts left on the far bank, nobody to tell tales to Adolf.

Ping. Ping.

P.B. extracted two riders. He didn't even have to think about it, not at a hundred fuckin' yards. Jesus, he could've done it in the fuckin' dark with his cock in a coalbag. Since the targets were still writhing on the cobbles where the ramp leaked into the road, P.B. used four more bullets to put them out of their misery.

One bike was still upright, the sidecar soldier fumbling to bring his gun into a firing position.

Ping.

The kraut flopped back and the machine dizzied on, bumped up on to the grass verge and fell over.

Before that happened, though, P.B. was on his feet, the Lee Enfield's butt light against his shoulder. He put the mag's last three .303s into the second sidecar soldier who, with one leg hooked over the rim of the car, was dragged for fifty yards, like an anchor, the combo still heading up the slope, held in line by the camber.

P.B. fitted a fresh magazine and swung.

Three krauts were in the water, out towards the middle of the canal, on this side of the wrecked bridge. Heavy disturbance in the water made them bob. Only one was conscious. Crying, arm raised, he appealed to P.B. to save him.

"Heil Hitler," said Corporal McNair and shot the waving kraut clean through the face.

He plugged the two who were floating on the surface, buoyed up on their coats like dead flounders. He gave them two apiece to be sure—which made seven.

Since he could see no more targets, P.B. scooped up the ammo and, holding his rifle at the port, started along the quay into settling dust and fine sepia-colored smoke. He heard shots. Not the Hotchkiss, though, which meant they had done it nice and clean and the lieutenant hadn't panicked. In the water P.B. noticed another floater, close against the steaming rubble of the blown piles. He gave the floater two—which made eight out of twelve.

P.B. walked on along the sunlit quay.

The two motorcycle combos which had cleared the bridge were hardly damaged at all. There was another one, if they could get their hands on it, tangled in the spars way out past the middle of the bridge. The three other German machines had gone into the drink and sunk without a trace. Except for the sounds of birds scared up by the racket it was quiet again. Quite distinctly P.B. could hear the slap of ripples against the banking. He smiled as he ambled along the promenade, the rifle warm in his hands.

Buz was prowling about by the water's edge below the cottage, the Bren at his side. The lieutenant had stayed up by the fox-hole with the machine gun, taking no chances.

Buz said, "How many?"

"Eight," said P.B.

"I got three. We've lost one," said Buz. "Where the hell's the last of 'em?"

P.B. thought it more than likely one of the krauts had been dragged down to the bottom of the canal, trapped in a sidecar.

"Yeah," said Buz, as if he had read P.B's mind. "He's most likely at the bottom. Wish I could be sure, though."

The lieutenant called, "What's wrong?"

"We lost one."

The lieutenant stepped over the barricade and picked his way down on to the quay. He had the Webley in his right hand, cocked and held up; like fuckin' Errol Flynn, thought P.B. Action didn't seem to have shaken Deacon, though. He seemed half asleep as he went past P.B. to the motorcycles sprawled on the road, stepping over the dead krauts as if they were puddles.

Buz continued to comb the bank for the missing German while P.B. went over to help the lieutenant with the bikes, heavy BMW R11s, 746 cc jobs with commercial sidecars bolted to the frame. One of the sidecars was badly battered but the machines themselves were intact.

"Can you ride a motorcycle?" the lieutenant asked.

"Never tried," said P.B.

"In that case the answer's no," said the lieutenant. "We'll strip off the car and take one solo bike and one combination. I wonder how much gas is in the tanks."

P.B. stood to one side as the lieutenant straddled the BMW and fired the engine, revving savagely. He squirted the bike forward and along the quay past the sergeant, on down the dirt towpath for three or four hundred yards, handling the brute well, then he braked and swerved and swung the combo round, the belly of the sidecar grating on the ground, and spurted back, one arm raised, shouting, "There he is. There he is. The missing kraut."

P.B. needed no second invitation.

Sprinting down the towpath, passing Buz on the way, he ran past the combo which the nance had abandoned, all three of them running down the canal now, until P.B. spotted the kraut in the water. The German was swimming like a porpoise, lunging head and shoulders up, disappearing under a vee of ripples and trail of bubbles. Some tough nut, P.B. thought, still wrapped up in a heavy greatcoat, booted and all, swimming like he planned on going all the way to the sea. For one fleeting moment the Scot no longer felt hatred and contempt for the enemy. He recognized a hard man, a survivor, when he saw one, even if he was a kraut.

Realizing he had been spotted, the kraut went under again, stayed under for as long as it took P.B. to pitch himself on his belly, find a prop on the verge for the muzzle and take first aim.

"Stay under, Jim," P.B. muttered. "Don't be fuckin' daft."

Buz and the lieutenant were crouched on their knees behind him, breathing heavily. They said nothing to distract him, however.

They all watched the water.

The kraut had been under for almost a minute.

"There," said the lieutenant.

The swimmer surfaced in a swooping motion, close against the canal's far bank. The mud was steep and black and gave no grip. He tried once, treading water, slithering to gain purchase, to reach his hands up to the bank. It was desperate, hopeless, the poor bastard hadn't a chance.

"Take him, corporal," said the lieutenant.

P.B. did not fire.

He could take him any time.

He watched the soldier go down again, swimming underwater along the line of the bank.

When the kraut surfaced again he did not even turn towards the slippery bank. He trod water and jutted one arm defiantly into the air in the Nazi salute. This one had no use for mercy, not him.

"Shoot him, corporal," the lieutenant ordered. "What's wrong with you? Can't you do it?"

Under his breath P.B. said, "Fuck off."

He drilled the swimmer cleanly through the forehead with a single shot which, he imagined, was what the courageous bastard had been begging for right there at the end.

"Well done, corporal."

The lieutenant patted his shoulder.

At that moment P.B. McNair hated the poncy officer worse than he hated the krauts. He lay where he was on the grass pad at the end of the towpath staring at the bubbles on the brown water.

Behind him he heard Buzz say, "Well, that's the lot accounted for."

And the lieutenant say, "Good. Now we can be on our way."

"Come on, wee man," Buz dug him with his foot. "Up an' at 'em."

"Aye, right," said B.P. and, rather wearily, pushed himself to his feet.

Twenty minutes later, having laboriously manhandled the BMWs across the spars of the lock arm, Deacon, Campbell and McNair dressed themselves in the bloody coats of the enemy and changed their profiles with blunt SS steel helmets. They mounted the cycles and weaved back down the towpath on the east bank until they reached the empty road and swung, unchecked, towards the town of St. Félice.

The lieutenant permitted P.B. to ride along with Buz. Crouched in the sidecar with a full, uncorked bottle of red wine among the mound of gear in his lap, P.B. cooled his ire with swigs from the bottle and, a couple of miles out of Quern, rocking and swaying like a bairn in a cradle, fell comfortably asleep.

3 Out of the frying-pan

MORPHINE, THE GREAT COMFORTER, held Phil Paget snugly in its arms. The needle had removed his pain and with it all sense of responsibility. Relaxed, he lay on a plaid blanket on a palliasse on the floor of the old corn pit and let the children of France look after his fate. Children they were too, hardly one of them over twenty except the horse-doctor, Georges, who was a bouncy little fellow with a gigantic brown moustache. Georges must have been thirty if he was a day, practically senile compared to the majority of combatants that Paget had so far encountered in this dashed war. Not even regular injections of morphine could dull Paget's gloomy realization that, at forty-four, he was well over the hill and had no business to be here at all.

It had been a mad mission from the start, the "bright idea" of some genius in the Defence Department. It was ironic that he, Phil Paget, had been chosen to go because he was the *youngest* member of the Birmingham team. Of all the senior members of the secret research group involved in the development of the Magnetron, he knew least about what was happening in Europe. For two years he had been crouched over a slide rule and wiring diagrams, concerned only with perfecting a high frequency transmitting valve, a cavity resonator which would expand the applications of Radio Direction Finding.

Why some Defence Committee bod felt it necessary to woo French radio-beam experts to England—specifically Maurice Linhart—and incorporate them into the British scientific programme was more than Paget could comprehend. Why he had been selected to "approach" Linhart, who was notoriously antagonistic towards the English, by flying to Lille, and why it was

41

necessary to take him there by RAF monoplane, risking his neck and the security of the Magnetron project, were riddles to which he would never have answers now.

From the moment that the Miles Master two-seater had touched down in the field outside Lille, Paget had known that his mission was doomed.

The flight itself had been a hellish experience, the little plane, strafed by German fighters and shot at by ground batteries, had swooped over scenes of such chaos that a landing seemed impossible. Only the skill and daring of the pilot, another stripling, had got them to Lille in one piece.

The pilot's name was Nicholson.

Nicholson had shown no trace of fear, admitted no possibility of failure. He had chatted away in cheerful clichés.

"I say, that's a bit dodgy, isn't it, old man?" he would cry as a shell exploded within feet of the cockpit cover. "Missed again, Hermann. Stay behind after class. Tut-tut-tut! Hold on to your hat, old chap, time for a touch of the ducks and drakes. *Whee-woo!* Here we go. I say, Hermann, still with us? That's hardly cricket."

Shaking like a leaf, Paget had cowered in the rear seat and it was not until the plane touched down that he realized that Nicholson had been bawling at the pitch of his voice throughout the duration of the flight, yelling idiotic remarks as a release for his fears.

The airfield was strewn with wrecked French fighters, pitted with fresh craters and obscured by the smoke of sabotaged oil dumps. On the horizon, veiled by smoke, the city of Lille resembled a medieval frieze. The noise of battle deafened Paget, a cacophony of individual sounds which he could not identify but all of which seemed to herald his extermination.

"There's nobody to meet me," he shouted. "What do I do? How do I get through this to the Institute?"

"I'm not just a pretty face, old chap," said Nicholson. "I'm your guardian angel. Wheels should be waiting. Yes, there we are."

Not thirty yards from the end of the runway were an infantry captain and a comical little Berliet command car with a sloping bonnet, torn canvas hood and headlamps like a frog's eyes.

"Nicholson?"

"Yes."

"Holms told me to expect you at twenty hundred. You made good time."

"In spite of interruptions," said Nicholson. "Are you coming with us, captain?"

"'Fraid not. My presence is needed elsewhere. I've been protecting this contraption long enough. It's all yours now."

"Where are the Germans?"

"East and north-west of the city. Do you have maps?"

"Yes." Nicholson patted the breast of his flying jacket. "The Institute is on the Boulevard Vauban, close to the *bois*."

"I know it," said the captain. "We're holding there—at least we were—but the fighting has been very fierce. I wouldn't shilly-shally, if I were you."

"That bad?"

"Pretty hopeless. The city'll be gone by morning."

"We'd better have a crack at it," said Nicholson. "Just to make the trip worthwhile. What say, doctor?"

Numbly Paget nodded.

It was obvious that Nicholson was no ordinary RAF pilot and had been briefed by the mysterious Major Holms to nurse him through the mission.

"I'll try to find a couple of lads to guard the plane, but I can't guarantee its safety," said the infantry captain. "Not as things are."

"Grateful for what you've done already."

"Think nothing of it," said the captain. "How is Holms since they landed him with that funny department?"

"Practically invisible," said Nicholson.

"One more thing," said the captain. "I've been asked to tell you that if you get into hot water, head for St. Félice. It's quite a leg from here but Holms has friends there who'll keep an eye open for you. Plus a radio contact."

"Thought of everything, has old Pete."

"I wish he had," said the captain. "Cut along, old chap."

Nicholson had shepherded Paget into the passenger seat of the comic-opera Berliet and, with a wave to the captain, had roared the four-wheel drive vehicle across the airfield. Weaving between craters and wrecked planes he had driven out of an unguarded gate at breakneck speed and spun right on to the paved road that would lead them into the stricken city.

Now, drugged, free of pain, at rest, Paget could not accept that Nicholson's life had been snuffed out. During the one-and-a-half-hour sortie into the heart of Lille, the doctor had become infected with Nicholson's fantasy that he was immortal.

Now he was alive, and Nicholson was no more.

"Nicholson?" Paget shouted. Rolling on to his elbow, he directed his voice towards the sliver of sunlight that penetrated the floorboards overhead. *"Nicholson, get me out of here."*

The boy did not look at all like the flying officer. He was solemn and sallow and slender, whereas Nicholson had been chubby and cheerful with hair the color of a teddybear's fur.

The boy moved like a lizard. Appearing instantly at Paget's head he hissed, "No, no, monsieur. No talk. Please, no talk."

"Nicholson."

The boy, who could not have been much over fifteen, looked as if he might weep.

"Nicholson, Nicho—"

The boy put a hand across Paget's mouth and pressed down. It smelled, as everything smelled, of farmyards. Fear, embarrassment and uncertainty clouded the boy's eyes. The boy was not looking at him now, his eyes rolling upward at a little rain of dust that fell from the underside of the boards. Overhead there was stealthy movement. The boy's mouth hung open. He had small, perfectly even teeth, like a rabbit's, Paget noticed, and a round, tender underlip, the sort of lips that, on a girl, one would have wanted to kiss.

Even in feverish delirium, Paget's conscious mind revolted at this thought. He struggled. The boy pressed a forearm across his chest. The shower of mill dust had ceased.

Deep inside his brain, Paget distinctly heard Nicholson's voice, light but authoritative, say, "Steady, old chap. Steady."

And he understood.

He lay still.

The French boy did not know who was up there, prowling the floor of the deserted mill where they had brought him to be safe.

The boy stiffened at an audible bump upon the floor above, then relaxed when the girl whispered, "Pascal, *c'est moi.*"

"Lisa?"

"Oui, c'est moi."

Paget heard the metallic clang of a manhole behind and above him, the scrape of shoes on iron. At his head was a wall of corn sacks, pungent with age, rustling with mice, rats too perhaps, though the French boy had assured him that this was not so. At his feet was a brick wall. The corners of the narrow underground cell were mounded with dried husks. He had no idea where the mill was situated, whether it was within the town boundary or safe outside it. Many, many questions rattled around in his head. But he had not been lucid enough to ask, and had no French. The other boy—not Pascal—did not speak English at all.

Paget closed his eyes.

They were with him now, cramped into the corn pit. He could not see them without making a full twisting turn and his plastered thigh would not permit it. He found the voices soothing, low and rapid, making not one bit of sense to him, of course, whispering away in French. Corn sacks muffled sounds and absorbed the echoes. Except for the roof, they could hardly have designed a better hole to hide him in. He had food, but no appetite. Milk and water were brought to him—and morphine. Georges attended his healing. By the time his bones knitted and he was able to walk again, perhaps the war would be over and he would be free to return to England.

Lids drooping, body as weightless as a cloud, Phil Paget hovered on the edge of sleep, lulled by the voices of the children of France.

If he had understood the language, however, not even morphine would have calmed his fears; the news that Lisa Vandeleur brought to Pascal Fromont was very grim indeed.

"Sylvie is dead, Pascal." Lisa Vandeleur put her arm about the boy's shoulder. For the moment the Englishman was forgotten. "The Germans killed her early this morning. Mama has gone to the town hall now. You must be with your Mama at this time."

"How can Sylvie be—?" Pascal swallowed the choking lump of sorrow that clogged his throat. "The Germans would not—"

"She was captured last night in the library."

"Did they find the radio?"

"No."

"How did they know where to look?"

"Somebody told them, Pascal."

"But why?"

"Somebody who likes Germans."

"Where have they taken Sylvie?"

"The town hall. It was there that they—did it."

Pascal Fromont struggled to hold back tears. He was fifteen years old and thought of himself as a man.

"I will kill them," he said. "I will kill the Germans who did this to her."

"No, Pascal. You must look after your mother. You are all she has left now."

"Will Papa come back? Will they give him leave?"

"I cannot answer," said Lisa.

"Did they—did they—?"

"She was shot," said Lisa.

"Who would—?"

"The general, the one who came this morning."

"Then—then—I will kill him."

"You have done enough, Pascal."

"Does Georges know?"

"I've sent word to him."

"He—he loved her."

"Yes, I know. We all loved her."

"You must give me one of the guns."

"No," said Lisa sharply.

She pushed the boy from her and held him with one hand, at arm's length. They were close against the short iron ladder that descended from the floor above.

"Listen to me, Pascal. We will take revenge for Sylvie. If not today, tomorrow. For the moment, you must comfort your mother. She knows little or nothing of all this. She will be confused."

"Yes," said Pascal. "I must go to Mama. You are right, Lisa. Will they—will we be permitted to—to take Sylvie now?"

"When there is time," said Lisa Vandeleur, "and when the Germans have done what they have been sent here to do."

"All for him," said Pascal Fromont scathingly. "Why do we not—?"

"Because we made a promise."

"A promise to the English," said the boy furiously.

"Better than a promise to the Germans, Pascal."

"He does not look important."

"He is important enough for the Germans to go to a great deal of trouble to lure him out of England. It was a trap all along, Pascal. The professor, Linhart, was part of it. He had no intention of returning to England with Paget. He cooperated with German Intelligence."

"How did Linhart know about us?"

"He didn't. He couldn't have known. It is somebody else, somebody here in St. Félice. Pascal, I'm sorry I got you and Sylvie mixed up in all this."

"Sylvie would tell them nothing."

"Perhaps that is why she was shot."

"What can we do, Lisa? Will they take us all, one by one, as they took Sylvie?"

"No, Pascal," said Lisa. "It is the Englishman they want—and me. They know who I am, what I am doing. Someone gave them the information."

"But if they know that you—"

"Go to the town hall, Pascal."

"The curfew—"

"The curfew is over. The SS have begun a house-to-house search of the town. There are people in the streets. It will be easier to move about now."

"Will they come here?"

"Yes, I expect they will," Lisa answered.

"Then they will find him."

"No, Pascal. Not if you do as I say."

"Do you want me to deliver a message to Guy at the library? I can do that, Lisa. I will not be seen."

"Guy is no longer at the library."

"The radio—"

"The SS have detectors. We dare not use the radio now, unless in emergency. Guy put out a message to London, asking for assistance. I have a rendezvous at noon today. I hope only that the rescuers will not arrive too late."

"How will they get here?"

"We must trust them." She gestured at the man on the palliasse. "How is he?"

"More comfortable since Georges gave him the injection at five o'clock."

"Is he still fevered?"

Pascal did not answer.

Lisa saw that the impact of her tragic news was making itself felt. The boy had loved his sister dearly. Grief would make him useless. She prayed that he would not do anything rash. He had acted very bravely for a fifteen-year-old, doing all that she had asked of him with no other motive than to aid France and support his Papa, a gunner in the French army. Madame Fromont knew nothing of her children's involvement in the war against the Germans.

"Go carefully, Pascal."

"I will come back."

"No, stay with your Mama."

The boy reached his hands to the ladder. The lid that sealed the old corn pit was secured by a drop bar. He fumbled with it then, braced, turned to face Lisa again.

Tears were brimming in his eyes.

"If only they had taken me, not Sylvie."

"Would you have been as brave?" asked Lisa.

"I would surrender Paget now, if it would bring Sylvie back to us."

Lisa nodded. She sought his hand but Pascal drew away, thrusting his shoulder against the lid, then slithering up into the mill. He left the lid askew. His lack of caution dismayed Lisa.

Hastily she secured the cover and returned to Paget. She had brought fresh water for him and cheese and bread but he appeared to be sleeping comfortably and she did not waken him.

She leaned against the wall of corn sacks and stared up at the crack in the floorboards, at sunlight.

It was ten minutes to nine o'clock. Georges and Guy were out in the backstreets searching for another hiding place. Her Papa was at "his post" in the belfry of the Church of St. Jeanne, on lookout. Sylvie was dead. There were no others, except Vivien, her cousin, and Lisa did not know where Vivien had hidden herself.

Nine minutes to nine o'clock.

Overhead she heard the furtive scurry of a rat and, in the distance, the wail of a siren.

Paget snored, a smile upon his face.

In three hours she must make her way through streets full of Germans to the library building and wait there in the hope that London would send someone who would miraculously whisk Paget to safety.

She no longer believed in miracles. Like Sylvie Fromont she had been born in St. Félice, and, like Sylvie, it seemed as if she might die here, very soon. But what she would not do, no matter the cost, was yield to Sturmbannführer Staudt and his army of pigs.

In broad daylight the strength of the German armored divisions could be clearly seen, laid out across the plain of Ombreville. Travelling fast, tanks and support units formed regular patterns on checkerboard pastures and sown fields, engulfing villages, hamlets and isolated farms that stood in their way. Smoke and pale flame colored the scene. Only on the far north-western horizon, however, twelve or fifteen miles away, were there positive signs of fighting. Red and white tracers and the florets of artillery shells scored the azure sky while, above the sector, planes fought out deadly dog-fights as gently as butterflies.

Deacon bounced the bike off the high road. A lift of ground here gave him his first vantage point. Campbell followed, sidecar leaping over tussocks to the crest of the low hill. P.B. wakened with a start and glowered out over the panorama, scratching his stubbled chin like a bewildered primate.

"Big push, by the look of it," Campbell said.

"Well to the north of us, however." Deacon was more impressed by the sight of the panzer thrust than he pretended to be.

"Straight for Dunkirk," said Campbell. "They ain't even hanging round to mop up."

"Yet we've encountered nobody, nothing?"

"Whatever's coming up *this* road is going to be heavy."

"Do you think there's a start line?"

"Sure do."

"At St. Félice?"

"Possibility."

"There's certainly no sign of Allied soldiers on the retreat," said Deacon. "And we're only a couple of miles out of the town."

"Give me your glasses." Campbell dismounted.

P.B. made to clamber out of the sidecar but the sergeant stopped him. "Sit tight, wee man. I'm only going for a looksee."

P.B. nodded and sucked from the wine bottle.

Campbell picked his way through tall underbush towards two stunted trees that leaned away from the prevailing wind, bent, like direction markers, towards St. Félice. The sergeant looked huge and ungainly in the SS greatcoat. As disguises the German uniforms had a limited application. Up close, Deacon knew they would be rumbled in seconds. Campbell crouched by the trees, binoculars trained due east towards St. Félice.

P.B. continued to gurgle at the wine bottle.

Deacon hesitated then said, "Corporal, that's enough vino. I suggest you stow the bottle."

"Suggest?" said P.B. McNair.

"Order you to put it away."

To Deacon's surprise McNair obeyed him without argument. He corked the bottle, slipped it into his field-sack and threaded the straps. He lounged in the sidecar, arms folded, passively studying the progress of the panzer divisions on the plain below. At least the "wee man," as Campbell called him, had learned to take orders, even if he didn't much care for officers and gentlemen.

Campbell's low whistle summoned Deacon. Propping the bike carefully, he ran to the stance by the trees. The road was visible, the clustered houses of the town. There were more wooded areas than on the north side of the ridge; coppices and ponds, broken dirt country with small blackwater lakes and lentic ponds, also tanks and the smoking hulks of British and French lorries. One aircraft, its markings charred away, had crashed by the roadside close below, wings broken and fuselage fractured by a clump of willows.

"What is it?" asked Deacon.

"Hurricane."

"Poor devil!"

"Maybe he got out," said Campbell. "Anyhow we've got our own problems."

Deacon took the field-glasses and scanned the roadway.

"Problems indeed," he murmured. The road-block swam into focus. "How many heads?"

"Couple of dozen, plus dug-outs in back," said Campbell.

"All for my benefit?" said Deacon.

"Smells that way."

"Well, we can't drive in, pick up our parcel and say thank you very much," said Deacon. "And it's the devil of a long wait for nightfall."

"Too long," said Campbell. "By the look of it the krauts are swarming to the Channel. If you want to have any chance of getting your boy back to England we have about fifteen hours to winkle him out of the town and reach one of the ports."

"Yes." Deacon checked his wristwatch. "In fact, I have about three hours to rendezvous with my contact at the town library. Vandeleur may have been taken prisoner, or the building gone up in smoke, of course."

"We won't know that until we're inside the town," said Campbell.

"Any ideas, sergeant?"

Campbell took the glasses from Deacon and studied the German block for a couple of minutes, then rolled on to his elbows. "You really want my advice, sir?"

"Of course."

"Go home."

"That," said Deacon, "I won't do."

Campbell grinned. "Okay! First we dump the bikes. Sooner or later the SS OC is gonna get curious about why his patrol hasn't radioed in. Maybe he has already. He'll send out a bigger unit to look for them. If he's smart he'll put two and two together and figure a rescue mission is on the way."

"Perhaps we could use the German uniforms?"

"And get shot for spies if we're caught."

"Point taken," said Deacon.

"A ditch, a deep ditch, runs right along the roadside, past the back of the road-block," Campbell said. "Here, lieutenant, see for yourself."

Deacon studied the terrain through the glasses. He saw at once what the sergeant was driving at.

"If you follow the line of the hedges to that clump of trees, keeping your eye peeled for patrols, you can slip into the ditch only three, four hundred yards short of the block. Crawl from there."

"It's risky," said Deacon.

"The wee man'll be with you."

"Where will you be, sergeant?"

"In the woods on the other side of the road above the block. I'll take the krauts' minds off things long enough for you to shimmy past."

"McNair won't be awfully keen on that idea."

"P.B.'ll do what I tell him."

Deacon frowned. The terrain certainly favored a direct approach, particularly if a diversion kept the guards busy.

"What'd you say?" Buz Campbell asked.

"What sort of diversion?"

"I'll think of something."

"I don't want anything to happen to you."

"It won't," said Campbell.

"Splitting our force, such as it is, is a sensible idea, though," said Deacon. "Yes, I think the ditch might be the answer."

"Sure it is," said Campbell. "I'll try to make it to the library for noon. If I don't show, don't worry."

"And if we don't show," said Deacon, "find Vandeleur."

"What does he look like?"

"Like this, rather." Deacon shaped curves in the air with the palms of his hands.

"He's a girl?"

"He's a she, yes. Dark haired, aged twenty-two. Speaks first-class English. Tell her Jeff Deacon sent you."

"What if she won't take my word on it?"

"Tell her I'll see her after the war—at the Café d'Or."

"The Café d'Or. What's that, a code?"

"Sort of," said Deacon.

"Do we go with the ditch?" Buz Campbell said.

"Yes, we go with the ditch," Deacon told him.

Minutes later, bikes and German uniforms hidden in the brush, Campbell went off along the breast of the ridge and Deacon, with P.B. at his heels, descended to the hedge line south of the highway.

Keyed up, Deacon led the Scot at a fast lick, moving in a half-crouch, head lifted to scout for guards in the meadow up ahead. Pistol, glasses and map were buttoned into his battledress blouse. P.B. had the Bren and his Lee Enfield. He trailed the guns expertly, arms hung out from his sides, wrists stiff.

The whitewashed wall of the block hut, a temporary structure that reminded Deacon of a Skegness beach cabin, showed through the leafy hedge. Guards sauntered around it, bored by an uneventful watch. Cloud crossed the sun, thin-ribbed bands that might bring rain later. Cattle browsed the untidy meadow. In the midst of ploughed land two crude scarecrows fluttered in a stir of breeze. Rooks and gulls peppered the dark brown earth.

Deacon reached the brush around the clump of willows. He dropped to his belly and crawled forward. P.B. was close behind him, on his belly too, the guns kept out of the moist grass by cocked elbows.

Deacon noted the disposition of the guards around the road-block. The barrier was a flimsy bar of wood topped with barbed wire hooked into two plugged posts. Erected by German sappers, it wouldn't have kept out a Ford Model T, let alone a tank. But it wasn't intended to, Deacon supposed. Its purpose was symbolic. The German commanders were confident that the Allies had been driven far from St. Félice. Scanning the lightly wooded hillside on the far side of the road he wondered what sort of show the Canadian would put on—a fire, a shooting, an explosion? Although he had only met Campbell that morning, he felt he already knew the Canadian well enough to expect something hot.

"Are you ready, corporal?" Deacon whispered.

"Aye."

"Keep your tail down and let's go." He holstered the revolver and crawled forward.

The weeds were rank, the ground soft beneath his knees. He propelled himself forward with a rowing motion of the elbows. The ditch was defined by a lush growth of weeds. Deacon went over the lip of the ditch like a crocodile. The walls were three feet high, the channel broad enough to allow him to lie comfortably on the bottom, in sour water and oozing mud. Cautiously he lifted his head and made a reconnaissance.

Deacon started as P.B. tapped his foot with the muzzle of the Bren gun and urged him on with a scowl.

Deacon rowed himself forward towards a sapling which grew close to the ditch, a hundred yards or so from the hut.

Glancing back again Deacon winked at P.B. who scowled blackly to show that he did not approve of this bloody nonsense.

Breathing through his mouth, Deacon settled against the wall of the bank and checked his wristwatch.

Nineteen minutes after nine o'clock.

Two hours and forty-one minutes to noon.

At that moment a dog bayed in the woods and the barrier guards shouted. Deacon was close enough to the hut to hear the sudden stampede of boots. More shouting.

P.B. punched Deacon on the buttocks. Deacon crawled forwards, head and tail tucked down, unseen and undetected.

The guards were fully occupied with the British soldier who had staggered down from the hill brandishing a white flag of surrender.

Sergeant Buz Campbell had given himself up.

Buz liked Deacon well enough but didn't trust him to see the sense in a plan which was, he had to admit, pretty vague. He was unconvinced that Deacon would ever find the French partisans or that the man he had to find was still alive. But Buz had been raised in a tradition of self-reliance that was part of the great Canadian heritage; he had gotten the lieutenant into St. Félice and, if he had luck, might even contrive to get him out again.

He was banking on it that the guards wouldn't shoot him on sight.

The white flag, a singlet tied to a branch, was probably a potent enough symbol to protect him. He hoisted it high above his head before he showed himself to the guns.

He yelled the only German words he had ever bothered to learn. *"Kamerad, Kamerad. Nich schiessen. Nich schiessen."*

When he heard the dog bay behind him in the woods behind the ridge, he got to his feet and waved the branch frantically.

The fear in his voice was genuine.

"NICH SCHIESSEN, NICH SCHIESSEN, NICH SCHIES-SEN," he bawled as he staggered downhill towards the guns that had swung in his direction. Involuntarily he broke into English. "DON'T SHOOT. DON'T SHOOT. I SURRENDER."

Sudden sweat completed the effect Buz had strived for, a crude cosmetic job of mud and thorn scratches, dirt rubbed into his face and naked chest. His battledress was ripped open, helmet discarded. Naturally he had flung away his weapons, except for a hunting knife, non-army issue, which was strapped under his puttee, and a penknife stuffed into his jockstrap. He looked about as defenceless as a guy his size could get.

"Kamerad, Kamerad, Kamerad."

Buz stumbled on to the road. He dropped the white flag and raised his hands high in the air. An officer and a couple of NCOs smirked before him. Troops circled him. He would be okay now. He risked a quick shuftie in the direction of the ditch, saw nothing there.

The SS officer had a suntan, lank blond hair and sugar-icing eyebrows. The officer jabbered and waved a Luger in his face.

Somebody prodded him in the kidneys with a rifle.

Somebody else, speaking bad English, demanded to know what regiment he was with.

"The Royal Langhams."

"Battalion?"

He told them.

The officer issued an order.

Buz was searched, briskly but not thoroughly. The knives were missed. He was prodded again. He had anticipated humiliation, was on guard against temper, put himself into a dull frame of mind, burning low as he was herded along the road by four troopers. The officer and a driver followed slowly in a light Opel field wagon.

Buz glanced at the ditch. No British arse wagged above the weeds. He put Deacon and P.B. out of his thoughts for a while and concentrated on absorbing details of the Germans' disposition.

There was a mile of open country between the road-block and the first of the town's houses, odd little bungalows built of blue brick and painted timber. Way left was a factory or warehouse, stuck incongruously amid farmland. No bridges, no railway crossing. Church, left, a pub, French style, hard by the churchyard wall; an ugly monument on a plinth, a war memorial to the glorious dead of St. Félice, thirty fading names.

They were running him now, a jog-trot, the Opel pressing, the four troopers clashing around him.

The ditch had long gone, meandering off into a scummy pond with ducks in the reeds and six or eight fat white geese gabbling round it.

They came into the town by a road flanked by modern villas, trotting through an open square surrounded by flat-roofed shops. Evidence of war was here in plenty. Shattered windows, demolished gables, stumbles of brickwork, slates strewn on the cobbles. Evidence too of SS occupation. Armed soldiers were ranked at all the corners.

Sweat ran down Buz's body. With the sun gone, the morning was muggy. Underfoot, asphalt gave way to cobbles. Commercial buildings closed around him. The linking street came out into the municipal square. Patch of grass, statues, one arid fountain, a dozen German vehicles plus a few local cars and horseless flat carts. He was made to run on the pavement, while the Opel prowled abreast. The officer, for some crazy reason, was standing, like he was leading a triumphal procession.

Plenty Germans here. SS troopers. Christ but they looked efficient when you saw them up close. Even lads with stupid features and no chevrons were shifting crisply into position.

This outfit, the SS Totenkopf, meant business.

Rounding the inner edge of the park, Buz was steered to the steps of a four-storey building with a lot of gingerbread architecture. The town hall, he reckoned, had become the HQ of the occupying commander. The officer skipped from the Opel, signalled to two guards, who ran Buz up the stone steps and through a swinging door. Past two more guards in dress uniform. Down a wood-panelled corridor under a grand staircase. Down a tiled corridor. Out back of the building into a gloomy courtyard, penned by the windows of the offices of the hall.

"Halten."

Buz drew up, hands on his head. Sweating, chest heaving, he thought what a helluva place this would be for an execution.

Within a couple of minutes, brass strode out of the rear door into the yard. Two of them, a major and a general. The major was about Buz's age. He looked pale and weary. The general Herr Obergruppenführer—was the meanest-looking, fish-eyed sonuvabitch that Buz had ever seen in an army uniform. Maybe it was the broken nose, or the slit-like mouth, or the quirking of the woven leather cane in his gloved hand.

The major conducted the interrogation in fair English. Buz figured he knew the sort of questions the major would ask. The Germans were nervous about a relief force dropping out of the skies—how else could a unit get anywhere near this town?—and would grill him on why he happened to be wandering about in the woods three days after the war had swept away towards the English Channel.

Buz's guess was right. He trolled out lies he had made up during the run, told how he had fought with the langhams at Besserac, how he had been left for dead when the panzers overran the town, how he had gone out at night to try to rejoin his regiment, how he figured he'd gotten lost.

What day was it?

The major told him.

"Christ!" Buz said. "I've been three days without food. No wonder I'm starving."

The general spoke to the major. The major asked Buz why he was fighting with a British regiment. How many Americans— Canadians—were with the Royal Langham Rifles? Buz said how he had been a regular soldier for six years and had come over to England to join the army because there was no work in Canada.

The major relayed it all to the general, including a whole lot more crap that Buz invented. He put on the stiff-upper-lip act, though, when the major started in on how many Americans and Canadians were fighting with the British.

"No, sir." Buz shook his head. "Can't tell you that."

"Will you tell me the name of the man you have been sent here to find?" said the major.

Buz let his features sag. "Uh?"

"It is true that you have been sent here to find one of your colleagues, also a spy."

"Spy? Jesus! I'm no fucking *spy*. Listen, I don't even know where the hell I am. *Spy?* I'm a bloody infantry sergeant. All I came in for was something to eat. I'm starving to death."

"We know that you are spy."

"Will you cut that out!" said Buz, allowing fear to show again. "Do I *look* like a spy?"

The major licked his upper lip. He was on the point of asking another question when the general intervened, brushing the major to one side with the leather cane.

Buz's dry mouth became even drier. It had not occurred to him that he might be mistaken for Deacon's missing person. If the Nazis were desperate enough to tie up an SS division and put a general in charge of the show then they wouldn't hesitate to torture the truth out of him. Didn't they know who they were looking for, even? Didn't they have photographs of the guy?

God help me if he happens to be a Canadian, six-six in height, weighing in at two hundred and ten pounds, Buz thought.

The cane caressed Buz's jaw. He winced, fists bunching. But there was no blow, no savagery. His head was held back and up while the general scrutinized him closely.

Without turning, the general spoke, an order.

Buz heard the sounds of a soldier dashing off to do the general's bidding.

The general spoke again. To Buz's surprise, the major came from behind and offered him a lighted cigarette.

Oh, Christ, they're going to shoot me.

Right here and now.

No quarter, no messing about, no trial.

Execution.

The first drag on the cigarette gummed Buz's lips together. He coughed, then gagged. For an instant he was paralyzed with terror. If he could be sure they had sent out for a firing squad, that the gesture of the cigarette meant what he thought it did, then he would bolt. He would grab the fucking general by the throat, use him as a shield. He would take one of the bastards . . .

The general laughed and passed a remark to the major.

Buz forced himself to drag again on the cigarette.

Still chuckling, the general took Buz by the arm, turned him and led him back towards the glass door in the wall of the building.

There was some kind of backlight, a sheen cast by linoleum or polished white tiles. Buz couldn't see properly. All he knew was that they were walking him towards somebody who stood behind the glass door, somebody who held his life on a string.

He stared at reflections, lattices of light and glassy shadow, the cigarette dangling from his lips.

Three yards short of the door the general stopped him. Gloved fingers pinched the cigarette and lifted it away. Again the touch of the leather cane, directing his head. Then, in the town hall corridor, a soldier shifted position and cut off the light. Buz stared into the face of a young girl.

She was small and pretty.

Buz stared straight at her, willing her not to denounce him.

As if in answer to his unspoken message, the girl shook her head. Immediately the general lost interest in Sergeant Buz Campbell.

It was left to the major to get rid of him.

Minutes later Buz was hustled through the town hall corridors, out into the square. People had gathered as if for a mass meeting. French folk, the citizens of St. Félice, men, women, children. Some were in nightgowns, others in working clothes. They were all confused and afraid.

Buz had no time to make an evaluation. He was bundled into a truck by two guards and the truck took off. It hauled out of the square and cornered into a side street from which more bewildered townsfolk were being herded.

Buz closed his eyes for a second, breathed deeply to calm

himself. One of the guards was leaning over the rail of the truck, laughing and cooing at the girls in the trail of civilians. The other, older, grimmer and more conscientious, was braced in a corner with his gun held steady. Buz kept his eyes closed. He thought better that way.

Who was she? Who the hell was she?

Lisa Vandeleur, working for the krauts?

Somebody back there at the end of Deacon's wire had sure screwed up. He wasn't the only guy who had underestimated the Nazis.

Opening his eyes Buz sullenly fell to assessing the lie of the land for the rest of the ride to Melampyre Farm.

The blonde mademoiselle spoke sufficient German to make herself understood without having to resort to Staudt's translations. In contrast to the girl that Ribbeck had dealt with earlier, this one was all tongue and eyes, a silly flirt. It irked the general to have to be gracious, to flatter and cajole, pretend that he was impressed with her sentimental platitudes and eager affirmations of loyalty to the Reich. On such fools, however, the fate of campaigns hinged. Ribbeck did not bully her. If it turned out that Mademoiselle Vandeleur was another trickster, or if she proved to be lying, the Obergruppenführer would turn her over to eight or ten hand-picked "volunteers," the biggest and roughest of his troopers, and let them have sport with her. He doubted if she would still be flitting her eyelids and pursing her sweet little red mouth at the end of it.

The Obergruppenführer removed his hat and gloves and settled himself in the chair behind the desk of the Inspector of Food Producing Animals. The office was on the ground floor to the rear, tucked away from the noise of the square. Mademoiselle Vandeleur would, he felt, appreciate the attentions of a high-ranking German officer. Ribbeck, however, was a cautious man. He had taken the precaution of borrowing a Luger from Staudt. The gun, loaded, rested in an open drawer of the inspector's desk on top of a bundle of typed forms pertaining to the health of dairy herds.

The girl perched on a straight-backed chair. She had pert high breasts, shapely legs and bubbly blonde hair tied with a pink ribbon, every soldier's dream of a French girl. She must have bowled over Private Otto Kress of the *Schutzen* regiment of the 5th Panzer Division who, Mademoiselle Vandeleur blushingly explained, had been her lover for six months in Munich, before the war. Ribbeck supposed that he should be grateful to Private Kress for corrupting the French provincial, politically as well as sexually. Kress had won her over to the cause of the Reich, cock being more important than country to females of this calibre.

Without Vivien Vandeleur's telephone calls, Military Intelligence would have known nothing of Paget's whereabouts.

Vivien Vandeleur had betrayed her country, her family and friends. The only shame, Ribbeck thought, was that she had not made a more professional job of it.

The Obergruppenführer said, "It was you, was it not, who made the anonymous telephone calls to Monsieur Conradin?"

"Yes, sir, it was."

"Why did you choose to call him?"

"I knew that he was—was a supporter of the Führer."

"Why did you choose to remain hidden?"

"Because I was afraid."

"Why then did you come forward this morning and make yourself known to us, at, I might add, a most opportune moment?"

"Because of what—what happened to Sylvie Fromont."

"Yet, if I am not mistaken, it was *your* telephone call to Conradin that told us where to find Sylvie?"

"I did not know it would be Sylvie."

"You thought it would be Lisa?"

"Yes."

"If we had found Lisa there instead of the Fromont girl, if Lisa had met with an unfortunate accident, would you be here now?"

"Lisa is an agent of the British. She works for an English major."

"So you told Monsieur Conradin who, of course, reported it to our Intelligence department. What you neglected to inform Monsieur Conradin was how you know that your cousin works hand-in-glove with the English?"

"She told me so."

"Did she not also tell you to come here today to confuse us further?"

"No, no, Herr General. No, I swear she did not. If Lisa—if they knew it was me, they would kill me."

"Did Lisa Vandeleur not send you to this office immediately it was learned that we had taken a prisoner? Were you not instructed to lie to us by telling us that the prisoner was not the man that we seek?"

"How could they send me here? They do not know that I—that I have told you *anything*."

"The prisoner we showed you—"

"He is not Paget."

"Ach, so you *have* seen Paget?"

"No, but he is wounded, very seriously. He cannot walk."

"Why should I believe you? You lied to the Sturmbannführer about Lisa Vandeleur being in the library. It was not her but another. And there was no man with her."

"I am not one of the librarians."

"What do you do?"

"I am a teacher of small children."

"Here, in St. Félice?"

"In St. Omer."

"Why are you here at this time? Why are you not teaching these small children?"

"School closed when the war came."

Ribbeck said, "Are your parents living?"

"No, they are dead."

"How long have they been dead?"

"Seven years, my father. Four years, my mother."

"Have you no sisters or brothers?"

"My brother lives in Paris now. He was one year in Munich, teaching the French language. It was there I met—"

The Obergruppenführer, who had already heard the boring tale of romance, interrupted. "Why did you return here and not go to Paris to be with your brother?"

"My Uncle Charles, Lisa's father, sent for me."

"How long ago did he send for you?"

"One week ago."

"Why did he send for you?"

Vivien Vandeleur laughed bitterly. "To make me into a spy. He did not know about my Otto. Perhaps Lisa would have stolen Otto away from me as she stole Henri—"

The bickering of vacuous schoolgirls, the ranklement of jealous children; so the girl Lisa had stolen a boyfriend from the girl Vivien, and Vivien would betray her out of revenge. It was more ruthless in its way than manly wars with tanks and shells and bayonets.

The girl prattled on about her emotional turmoil, how she had suffered when Lisa had "taken Henri away." Ribbeck cared not who Henri was. He stifled his impatience. He could have wrung this idiot dry within minutes. She would not act as the girl had done this morning. But he could not alienate her yet. She might still be useful.

"I see," he intervened. "Did the Vandeleurs not tell you where the English airman, Paget, is hidden?"

"After I refused to join with them to help the English, they told me nothing."

"How unfortunate."

"But I know that Paget is with them, hidden somewhere in St. Félice. They are waiting for the English major to send in a force to take him away."

"How do you know this?"

"The son of the woman with whom I lodge, she told me."

"Does she trust you?" Ribbeck inquired.

"She does not understand."

"Does not understand what?"

"About Lisa and I."

"How does the woman with whom you lodge obtain her information?" asked Ribbeck.

"From her nephew."

"What is his name?"

"Guy Leconte."

"Where is he to be found?"

"Madame Leconte does not know. She has not seen him since Tuesday."

"What other names have you heard?"

"From Madame Leconte?"

"From anyone," said Ribbeck.

"Only Georges Bergier."

"Who is he?"

"A surgeon for horses."

"Ach, he may be the person who doctors the Englishman. Where is this Georges to be found?"

"He was employed by the Kobiela family to attend their thoroughbreds but the Kobiela family took all the horses away from here to the south, to Nice I think, when Poland was—was put under your command."

"But they must be somewhere, these people—your uncle, your cousin, Leconte and this horse-surgeon."

"Nobody knows where they are hiding."

"Have you tried to find out?"

"Yes, Herr General, but I am treated with suspicion by the friends of my uncle, those who support the English."

"How did they become agents of the English?"

"There is a man in London, a major."

"Name?"

"Holms."

"Go on, mademoiselle, please."

"The Major Holms' father fought with Charles Vandeleur in the last great war. Ten months ago, the father and the son came to St. Félice and stayed with Charles. Lisa, I have heard, went back to London with them for a short while then returned here."

Ribbeck was impressed. He wondered if the *Abwehr* had collected any information about the Holms and their spy nest. It would give him extreme pleasure to present a discreet and detailed report to Herr Hitler which would surely bring down the Führer's wrath on the career officers in the *Abwehr*, those men who had had the gall to concoct a dossier on his, Josef Ribbeck's, private life and criticize the wisdom of his appointment to high office simply because he selected nice young officers for his staff.

The blonde fuddlewit was proving very valuable.

Cocking his head, the general questioned her further about Holms and his spy network. The girl's information was woolly. Even so, he now had a list of names to work with. His disappointment at not laying hands on Paget waned a little. Delay had worked to his advantage. But now it was time to tighten the screw.

Ribbeck brought the questioning to a close.

"Have you no clue as to where the Englishman is hidden?"

"Oh, no, Herr General. But he is somewhere in town, of that I am sure."

"Why did you tell me that he might be found in the library?"

"They are mostly librarians. Archivists," said Vivien Vandeleur. "Do you not know that the library of St. Félice is famous for its collection of books and manuscripts on the history of warfare? My Uncle Charles, he is an expert, and Lisa received training in London. She had been many times to London."

"Is it, do you think, to the library that the English will come to make contact?" said Ribbeck.

He was aware that it was a long shot but he had no other immediate use for the girl. It was improbable that Lisa Vandeleur or her friends would ever allow the blonde to discover anything of value.

The girl said, "Yes—to the library."

"Where contact will be made?"

"Yes."

"That contact will be you, mademoiselle. I will keep my soldiers out of sight, to help lure the English—if they come at all—to get in touch with you. When they do, you will bring them to me. Do you understand?"

"Yes, Herr General. But—"

He detected concern in her blue eyes. He said, "I give you my word as a German officer that you will be taken care of when the business is done."

Ribbeck got to his feet and put his arm about her shoulder. She fluttered her eyelids at him.

"How would you like to marry your Otto?" Ribbeck asked.

"Marry Otto? But he is at the Front, fighting."

"You will have a passport to take you to Munich. Leave will be arranged for Otto, two weeks or three. It is not difficult. Germany can afford to lose the services of one soldier for a little while, in the cause of love."

"How can I thank you, Herr General?"

"Do as I have told you, little one, and that will be thanks enough."

Ribbeck opened the door, called to the guard and issued instructions in rapid German; then he lifted Mademoiselle Vivien's hand and kissed it, clicking his heels. Still holding her hand, a final thought occurred to him.

"By the way, who was the girl; Sylvie Fromont?" he said.

Vivien Vandeleur simpered and shrugged. "Nobody of importance," she said.

Deacon wished that the big Canadian was with him now. True, he did have P.B. McNair. But the Scot was a disciple not a leader and Deacon was suffering a loss of confidence in coping with this Alice-in-Wonderland situation. On the positive side, though St. Félice was occupied, the SS unit was thinly spread and he was able to lead McNair out of the ditch and into the cover of cottage gardens without undue risk.

There might be unfriendly eyes in any of the garret windows, of course, or some Frenchman motionless in the shade of the hedges; Deacon dared not permit himself to become *that* paranoid. He kept on the move.

It was, he thought, rather like climbing a new route in the Alps. One had to be conscious of the overall line, yet focus on the sequence of holds immediately within reach. Scuttling along the backs of the hedges in the little French town, Deacon held panic at bay. Rhythm, that was the thing. Intelligent forward motion. Beitzke, his climbing guide and mentor, had taught him that valuable lesson during his first visit to Innsbruck, when he was fifteen years old. Beitzke was an Austrian with no love for the Germans; he wondered, as he plunged on, what had become of the grizzled old guide.

Rhythm. Balance. Forward motion.

Blank out negative possibilities.

Free of the trap of the ditch, upright and making progress, Deacon began to feel better.

Behind him, McNair moved with enviable lack of effort, lugging two heavy weapons.

Common sense told Deacon that if he could skirt the arterial roads, he would find better cover close to the town center. To reach the library in the Boulevard Sainte Barbe, however, was not going to be easy.

Leaving suburban houses behind, Deacon found his route blocked by a high brick wall. Weathered signs told him it was a corn mill. No gate opened from the yard wall which was several hundred yards long. The building had smashed windows, rusted gutters and broken slates and was obviously deserted. To the right, at the wall's end, little old stone houses crowded close upon a raised earth bank. Deacon knew where he was now. Skirting the base of the wall he started out for the earth bank, part of the town's ancient defences.

P.B. grabbed his arm.

"Why did y'let him go?"

"What?" Deacon's mind was on other things.

"Buz. Why didn't y'stop him?"

"It was his idea." Deacon wrenched his arm away. "Besides, I didn't imagine he would give himself up."

"Got t'get him back."

"Look here—" Deacon began, then, seeing black rage in the Scotsman's face, thought better of argument, and nodded.

"How then?" said P.B.

"We'll find him," said Deacon, "I promise you, after we've accomplished—"

"Fuck that," said McNair. "I'm goin' t'find Buz *right now.*"

"The devil you are."

"Aye, what's t'stop me?"

"A couple of hundred Germans, for a start," said Deacon. "In addition to the simple fact that you haven't a clue where they've taken him."

P.B. sulked, the Bren on the ground, the Lee Enfield slung across his shoulder. "They'll have taken him for questionin'."

"In which case," said Deacon, "they'll have him somewhere in the center of town. So, corporal, I suggest you stick with me for the time being."

"Ach!" said P.B., disgusted at defeat by logic. "Bugger it!"

And he picked up the Bren gun, following Deacon along the length of the wall.

Distracted by McNair's outburst, Deacon almost walked into a German patrol. Eight foot-soldiers, supported by a panzer-wagon, were herding a crowd of French civilians towards the town center. Thirty-five or forty citizens, including children and infants in arms, were being driven like slaves to the block.

Only a straggle of privet screened Deacon from the Germans. P.B. pulled him back.

Lying side by side in a trough formed by the mill wall and the earth bank, the pair waited, guns at the ready, while the sounds of the troupe diminished.

Cupping his hand to his mouth, Deacon whispered, "The krauts are clearing the streets. I suspect they intend to make a door-to-door search."

"What'll they do with the Frogs?"

"Herd them into a church, I expect."

"Where's Buz? Same place?"

Deacon did not answer. He crawled up the bank, surveyed the narrow street, rose and ran across it and dived into the doorway of one of the houses.

Close as a leech, P.B. followed.

The Germans had done them a favor. With the houses empty there was no shortage of cover. Deacon pushed on through a tiny corridor, found a kitchen door and went through it into a patch of garden at the end of which a low stone wall defined a lane between the cottages. Deacon vaulted the dyke. Turning, he glimpsed a withered face peering out of a window, a face which vanished like the visage of a ghost. Next he caught sight of a bare-legged boy running down the lane. Fleet as a deer the boy disappeared into a garden. Deacon started along the lane with P.B. trotting at his heels. At last he was travelling in the right direction towards the town's tall steeples.

Six hundred yards further on, at the lane's end, Deacon encountered the enemy.

The privates were sneaking a cigarette and sharing a bottle of local beer. They had been posted to guard the debouchment of three roads, stationed under the gridded windows of an almshouse, a building preserved from the seventeenth century about which the aura of poverty and pessimism still clung. Beneath their steel helmets the soldiers looked like what they were, bumpkins lucky enough to conform to the SS image. Their carbines rested against the wall, while the beer bottle, a blue glass flagon, passed from hand to hand.

Deacon was out of the lane before they saw him, if they saw him at all. Shots rang out. The soldiers fell. The blue glass flagon dropped between them and exploded on the flagstones like a grenade. Echoes of the shots sang in the humid air.

"Better hide them." McNair lowered the Lee Enfield. "Stick'm in the auld house, right?"

The soldiers lay as if drunk. One had been drilled between the shoulder blades, the other through the chest.

"C'mon, c'mon," said McNair impatiently. "Maybe somebody heard the shots."

With the rifle in his left hand, McNair kneeled and expertly looted the Germans' pockets. He came up with cigarettes, a bar of chocolate and a fistful of franc notes, which he stowed away in his webbing pouch.

"Here, take the Bren an' cover me," said McNair.

Deacon accepted the weapon. He rested his shoulders against the pebbled wall and watched McNair drag the corpses one by one through the open door of the almshouse. On the flagstone there remained only patches of blood, fragments of glass and the butt of a cigarette from which smoke still wisped. The cobbled streets remained empty, the lane too.

Deacon cursed himself for lack of caution. If the soldiers had been more alert he would have been dead by now. Only McNair's reaction had saved him. Deacon knew he should be grateful, but he was not. He had lost face and authority.

Wiping his hands on his buttocks, P.B. emerged from the oak door, closed it quietly and picked up the Lee Enfield. He took the Bren gun from Deacon as if it was a dangerous toy that Deacon was too irresponsible to be allowed to keep.

"Where to, then?" said McNair.

"This way."

"D'you really know where we are?"

"Yes," said Deacon. "As it happens, I do."

Moving with more stealth, Deacon started along the side of the almshouse, keeping a weather eye on a burial allotment which lay, behind railings, adjacent to the street.

At the end of the street a little church split the prospect. To the right of the church Deacon could make out the edge of the town square crowded with civilians and SS troopers. The left fork ran past the kitchen-yard of an inn, a half-timbered building flanked by a modern brick block.

A truck rounded a corner of the square.

P.B. was already halfway across the street towards the corner of the burial lot. He swarmed over the spiked railings and ducked into the cover of the shrubs. Deacon followed him.

Crouched low, they watched the truck rattle past. It was heading out of town, due south.

"Christ! It's Buz. They've got Buz in yon lorry," said P.B.

"Well, at least we know he's safe," murmured Deacon.

Campbell was seated in the back of the truck. Two armed soldiers guarded him.

"They'll be takin' him t'Germany."

"I doubt it," said Deacon. "I expect there's a transit camp somewhere on the edge of town."

"Aye," said P.B., grinning. "Aye."

The truck had passed out of sight.

P.B. McNair was on his feet.

"I'll be seein' you, sir," he said.

"You can't—"

"Cheerio."

The corporal was gone before Deacon could stop him. Darting through the shrubs, across the angle of the burial lot. P.B. sprinted out of a gate in the railings between the trees, heading, of course, south out of town. With him he took the rifle and the Bren, leaving Deacon with no weapon except his revolver.

"Dear God!" said Deacon under his breath, then, after a moment's pause, pushed on alone towards the rear of an inn, Le Pelican.

* * *

Perched on top of a tank that Ribbeck had ordered from the bullring, Staudt did not feel like a conquering hero. The tank was ominously poisitioned by the town hall steps. Frightened French peasants, almost the entire population of St. Félice, packed the square. In spite of armed soldiers, machine guns and the presence of tanks, Staudt realized that if the citizens of St. Félice elected to rebel, sheer weight of numbers would overwhelm his forces. But the French did not know it. For that he had to be thankful.

Staudt peered at the orders Ribbeck had written, orders he was expected to translate and deliver.

He put the megaphone to his lips.

"Attention. Attention. *Garde à vous*."

The crowd shuffled, drawing closer, as Staudt announced the general's demands.

The demands were simple; certain men and women were to be handed over to the Obergruppenführer at once. The reading of each name gave rise to gasps and mutterings in the crowd.

Staudt ignored the reactions, pressing relentlessly on. "Charles Vandeleur. Lisa Vandeleur. Guy Leconte. Georges Bergier."

Staudt proceeded to inform the people that a stranger was hidden in their midst, a wounded Englishman, and that he too must be handed over, alive, to the Obergruppenführer.

"Anyone found harboring or aiding this person will be dealt with harshly," the major read.

Staudt paused to scan the faces, wondering if Leconte or Bergier might step forward, play the martyr as the girl, Sylvie, had done, displaying the mad courage that was a civilian's only weapon against military might.

"If the Englishman is not found and handed over to us by one o'clock today," Staudt shouted, "twelve prisoners will be shot. The first dozen will include your Mayor, Town officer, and other municipal staff presently in our custody."

Subdued uproar; a gnarled old man close to the steps shook his fist and howled. Raging, a fat woman in a canvas apron waddled towards the tank only to be pounded upon by two soldiers and dragged bodily away.

"At three o'clock," Staudt went on, "twenty more prisoners

will be executed. Twenty selected at random. At five o'clock, thirty more, and so on until the Englishman is surrendered."

Wailings, cries of rage and terror rose up from the throng. The soldiers snapped rifle bolts and aimed into the swaying crowd. On the rooftops machine gun muzzles dipped. Glancing round, Staudt saw Ribbeck watching with approval from a first-floor window.

Staudt pressed the megaphone to his mouth.

"It need not be so," he declared. "If the Englishman is handed over to us, together with the traitors whose names I have read out, no blood will be shed. You will be permitted to return to your homes and continue your daily lives in peace, under the protection of the German army."

Staudt was not sure that he made himself heard above the hubbub. He was, however, certain that the people understood the nature of the ultimatum.

"In the meantime, until one o'clock, you will be kept here, and order will be preserved."

The Obergruppenführer had debated the wisdom of holding the population in the square. The town, however, was too sprawling to make a second round-up practical. Besides, with the houses empty, search details could push on with their work unimpeded.

"Order must be perserved."

Staudt repeated the general's final benediction and stepped down.

He checked the time on his wristwatch.

Almost ten.

He glanced at the sky. Thank God it had clouded over. The sun could be quite fierce and there were many babies and children in the crowd. He watched the crowd settle on the grass of the little park. There were few places to hide. One hundred armed soldiers could comfortably contain the gathering, huge though it was.

Staudt stepped back as the tank prowled off to a position on the corner of the Boulevard Sainte Barbe. The square's other entrances were also blocked by tanks, their 30 mm guns trained on the park.

The strategy was sufficiently ruthless to be effective. But it was a far cry from honest battle and Staudt was disgruntled by his part in it. Now there was nothing to do but wait, wait for the search to root out the Englishman, for the French to come to their senses and bring forward information about the Vandeleurs. Somehow—

cynically—Staudt did not imagine it would take long. Ribbeck was right: by mid-afternoon it would all be over and the Totenkopf would be on its way to Dunkirk.

Crouched below an open widow in a maids' dormitory at the top of Le Pelican, Deacon could hardly believe his ears as he listened to Staudt's announcement.

Whatever notions Deacon had formed of warfare they did not include the shooting of innocent civilians.

Paget must be more valuable than anyone at home realized. The Germans obviously thought so. Somehow, Deacon reasoned, I've got to let the partisans know I'm here. What I need is a show.

No flags, balloons or bunting. No explosives or grenades. Deacon rummaged in his pockets and brought out his petrol lighter.

The upper floors of the old Pelican Inn were timber framed.

Deacon chuckled and retreated from the window in search of kindling.

The farm at Melampyre was situated in pleasant countryside less than two miles from the town square. The guards had broken open the farmhouse and looted the family's silver trinkets and, in pique at the paucity of the haul, had smashed the handsome antiques that lined the living room and kitchen. With more purpose and excuse they had pillaged the larder and feasted well.

The stone barn made an ideal prison. It had only one door. A hay trap on the upper wall was secured with nailed timber. The door was barred from the outside. Occasionally the captain and a sergeant conduted a head count. The eighteen prisoners were all males, municipal dignitaries trucked in from town, plus three British servicemen who had been marooned during the fighting and had failed to evade the cast net of the Totenkopf. The morning had been uneventful, however, until the arrival of a new prisoner, a British army sergeant named Campbell.

The door clattered behind Buz. Bars dropped, a catch chain rattled. Buz studied the architecture of the place before giving his attention to the prisoners who had risen to greet him.

High, vaulted, beamed, with an upper floor; vent windows, most of them without glass, were too narrow to allow a man exit.

Buz pointed. "Is that the only way out?"

" 'Fraid so, old sport," said an RAF pilot officer.

"How many guards here?"

"Not sure, old sport."

"Has anybody thought to count them?" demanded Buz.

"We've seen eight," said an Armored Corps private. "How'd they get you, sarge?"

Buz ignored the question.

"How many soldiers have we got here?" he said.

"Three army," said the tank private, "and 'is nibs 'ere."

"I'm a pilot," said the RAF officer. "Senior officer here, actually."

"What about the rest of the prisoners?"

"All bloody Frogs," said an infantry man in a Newcastle accent.

"Any of you speak German?" said Buz.

"I do." A heavy-set, rubicund man in his late fifties pushed himself up from a straw bale. "I am Guizot, Mayor of the town of St. Félice."

"And you understand German?"

"*Oui*, a—a—trifle."

Buz said, "Enough German to pick up what's happening?"

Guizot shrugged. "They are here for to catch spy from England."

"The Frog's only guessin', sarge. He don't know no more than we do," said the tank private. "We been here since yesterday, when the Totenkopf took over from the Leibenstandarte."

"What other griff have you gathered?" said Buz.

"Precious little, I'm afraid," said the pilot officer.

"Then we've got to scare some up," said Buz.

Guizot had been joined by four other Frenchmen, plump officials. He would have introduced them one by one if Buz had given him a chance.

Curtly, Buz said, "I've come here to get you out."

The pilot officer said, "Don't tell me you dropped in for the express purpose of rescuing us?"

"That's the story," said Buz.

"Who dropped you?" asked the Geordie.

"I came in by road," said Buz, "through Quern."

"Quern?" said the private. "I've heard of Quern. Ain't it—?"

"Jesus! What part of your head did you land on, son?" Buz Campbell snarled. "What the hell's wrong with you? The town's been taken over by a special division of the SS. You think they're gonna ship you all off to a spa for the duration?"

"It won't be easy to get out of here," said the pilot officer. "Alive, I mean."

"Do the krauts have a routine?" asked Buz.

"Unfortunately not."

"How do they feed you?"

"We've only been fed twice."

"Bloody good tuck, though," said the Geordie.

"How did they dish it out?" Buz asked the pilot officer.

"Opened the door and pushed in three buckets of chuck, plus a couple of cans of water."

"What've we got by way of weapons?"

The PO shrugged. "Personally, I have nothing. We were all searched."

"And interrogated?"

"Grilled like sausages, man," said the Geordie.

"Monsieur," interrupted the Mayor, "it is my belief that if the Bosch do not find this spy they will use us as hostages. Shoot us, perhaps."

"Good Lord!" said the pilot officer. "Would they stoop to that?"

"Aye, man, the Frog's right. They're trigger-happy bastards, this lot," said the Geordie.

"I've got to find out how the land lies. Did anybody notice if they have a machine-gun post with a field of fire to include the front of the barn?" Buz glanced round. Other prisoners had gathered about him now, but there was no answer to his question. "No? Okay!"

"It was dark when they brought me in," said the infantry private, as if to excuse his negligence. "I was dead on my feet."

"You'll be dead on your back if we don't do something soon," said Buz. "I'm going to create a little hell."

"Oh-oh!" The pilot officer backed away from the door. "I don't think our German friends are going to like this."

Buz struck the barn door with the heel of his boot. He drew back and kicked again, roaring, "Where's the commandant? I demand to see the commandant." He fell against the door and beat on it with his fists. "Who's in charge round here? Christ, what sort of army you guys running? Lemme out, lemme out."

The startled cries of the guards, the sound of running feet, the smack of rifle bolts answered him. Buz did not slack off. He kept hammering on the door.

The door creaked, the bar scraped. Pulled from behind, the door opened an inch.

"What is the trouble, English?"

Thank God one of the krauts spoke his language.

"This's intolerable," Buz shouted. "I won't stand for this sort of treatment. I demand to see the commandant. Get me the commandant."

"Step outside," said the voice.

Hands raised Buz went into the daylight.

Eight carbines and two automatic rifles were trained on him. The captain was standing behind a dung cart with a Luger in his fist. Four of the carbines were tucked down behind a wall, the rest in the doorways of outbuildings.

"Step forward," said SS Hauptsturmführer Hanreich.

Buz measured ten paces from the barn.

A soldier rushed his shoulder against the barn door, closed and secured it and covered Buz from the rear.

"What is it you require?" the captain asked.

Buz measured another eight paces. He could see past the corner into the main yard now. Two bicycles leaned against the wall by the open door of a farm kitchen. Army issue socks were drying on a line. Chickens clucked unconcernedly across the flagged yard. Pigeons on the roof. No four-wheeled transport. A cook, like all army cooks, loitered by the side of the kitchen door, a skillet in his hand.

"Food," said Buz. "I need food. *Manger.*"

"There will be food for you soon, English. Be patient."

"I ain't eaten for three days," said Buz. "I'm starving."

"So much noise because you have an empty belly." The captain shook his head. "Is it not a saying that the British army walks on its stomach?"

"Yeah, a full stomach," Buz said.

If this captain was as smart as he looked, he would have six or eight men circling the barn to guard against the possibility that Buz had been sent out to create a diversion. But the captain, it seemed, was arrogant rather than astute.

Buz clutched the pit of his stomach. "Sir, I'm hurting for lack of food."

The captain came out from behind the dung cart.

"You are American?" asked the captain.

"Canadian."

"I have been in New York," said the captain. "Six months. My cousin, his wife, they lived in Brooklyn. You have heard of Brooklyn?"

"Sure," said Buz Campbell. "Nice place."

The captain studied him then spoke in German to the corporal who cut off across the side yard and passed a message to the cook.

"See," said the captain, "you will be comfortable while you dine. Sit on the wagon. I will not permit hunger to make you pain. There will be enough pain for you soon, perhaps."

"How come?"

"No, it is a jest," said the captain. "In Germany you will be treated well."

"Is that where you'll ship us—Germany?"

"What else would we do with prisoners of war? When we have won over England you will be given places in the new Reich—if you do not make trouble."

Buz said nothing. He was watching the farmhouse door. The guards hadn't changed position, hadn't slackened their vigilance.

"Be seated, sergeant."

Buz hoisted himself on to the flat car. The ammoniac odor of horse dung enveloped him. The SS corporal returned with a sandwich of rye bread, sausage and fried egg, and a tin mug full of black coffee.

"A feast, do you see?" said the captain. "It is jolly like at home?"

Buz did not reply. Stuffing the bread greedily into his mouth and swallowing, he sighed. He didn't have to act it. He had burned up a lot of energy since breakfast back by the Quern canal. He was genuinely hungry. He gobbled the sandwich and washed it down with coffee. The captain watched approvingly.

So far no other soldiers had shown themselves.

The land ran flat from the wing of the farm. Two lines of stake fencing marked a vegetable patch. There was a windbreak behind it, bushes dense with new foliage. And a pump and water trough of galvanized iron. Beyond that lay the fields. Low hills hemmed the horizon. There was sun on the hills, like gold paint, but the sky over St. Félice still wore a cloud lid.

"You are better?" inquired the captain.

"Yeah. Thanks."

"Go back then, with your comrades. It will be food time for all quite soon."

Buz got down from the cart. He hadn't learned too much though he had gotten a free meal and a drink of decent coffee out of the exercise. He moved towards the barn door which the SS corporal had opened for him.

"Sergeant?" the captain said.

Buz turned.

"Do not make noise again."

"Right," said Buz.

"Next time, no breakfast. Bullet."

"Right."

They were all looking at him, all concentrating on him. Nobody saw the stake rise up from behind the galvanized iron trough on the far side of the vegetable garden. Only Buz. Buz could not help but stare at it for a second until he got over his astonishment and willed himself to look away. He turned and strolled towards the open door, hands on his head, turned once from the waist just before he entered the barn.

"Thanks," Buz said.

The captain gave him a little bow, arrogant and ironic.

Buz didn't give a fuck about the captain. It took him all his time not to holler with relief.

The stake was still there, a peeled ash wand crowned with an empty wine bottle identical in shape, size and color to one Buz had last seen cradled in P.B.'s loving arms.

Coincidence?

No chance.

The wee man was on the loose.

4 Massacre at Melampyre Farm

IT TOOK DEACON TEN MINUTES to set the fire. He regretted the necessity of damaging such a fine old building but salved his conscience with the thought that the Pelican Inn would probably not survive the war.

In the fuel cellar Deacon found paraffin and four litre cans of petrol that the landlord had hoarded. Sweating, Deacon toted the cans up the back stairs and dumped them in the corridor outside the servants' dormitories, sparse rooms whose windows overlooked the square. He steered clear of public rooms and guest bedrooms; it was possible that SS officers might be billeted on the premises.

Once the fuel had been transported, Deacon went in search of a linen cupboard which he found without much trouble. He broke the lock, hauled out towels and bedsheets and carried them back to the dormitory. Quite by chance he also found flags—a Tri-color, a Union Jack and a Swastika. Immediately he felt less guilty about razing the inn; Le Pelican's proprietor clearly intended to present a pleasant face to everyone, regardless of politcal persuasion. The Union Jack and Nazi flag were big as bath towels. Deacon took them to the dormitory too.

Sheets, towels and bedclothing, soaked with paraffin, were mounded under the windows, mattresses from the six bedsteads dumped against the wooden walls. The gasoline was liberally sprinkled about the room and along the corridor. Finally Deacon soaked the Swastika with paraffin and, kneeling, opened two windows. He pushed out the Nazi flag and hooked the cords to the window catches. A faint breeze caught and tugged at the fabric, unfurled it. Crabbing, Deacon thrust the British flag through an adjacent window then quickly touched his lighter to a paper taper and ran flame in the mounded kindling. He watched it catch and ignite then, back-tracking, lit the gasoline trail out into the corridor.

It would have been satisfying to watch the effect on the Germans in the square below but Deacon was halfway down the kitchen stairs before the smoke was spotted. He went out by the kitchen yard, veered right and followed the street to a quaint shopping arcade. He went through the arcade, veered right again and halted at the corner of the square and the Rue Obelle.

Black smoke billowed from the top floor of the Pelican. The flags hung down, the Swastika rimmed with red flame, the Union Jack intact. If Lisa Vandeleur did not find meaning in that signal then she wasn't worth her salt.

As Deacon watched, tendrils of yellow flame licked from the open windows. Civilians were already streaming out of the park in the confusion and consternation of the guards who, without instruction, did nothing. Rifles, fired over the heads of the crowd, caused further confusion. Tension was released. Women screamed. Children wailed. Old men yelled for order and calm. An officer on the town hall steps was bellowing through a megaphone. Nobody paid him any attention.

Taking a last fond look at the burning, Deacon slipped away. He ran hard, fire bells cheering him on his way. By the time he reached the turning at the Pauline Convent he was beginning to feel decidedly confident again. Scuttling from doorway to doorway, he came to the corner of the Boulevard Sainte Barbe, fifty yards from the library. Stepping stealthily out from shelter he risked a reconnaissance of the street.

The library was a minute's walk away, a tall grim building with gridded windows and an arched doorway. To his right a bunch of German soldiers, clustered round a light tank, goggled at the activity in the square. Deacon stepped out of cover, walked boldly down the west side of the Boulevard Sainte Barbe, crossed the street, mounted the steps of the library and pushed his way in through the lead-glass portal.

The door thumped behind him. Dusty echoes stirred through the vaulted foyer. A high desk was backed by filing cabinets and a variety of notices. The musty smell reminded Deacon of Trinity

College. A clock with a tick like pebbles dropping into oil dominated the cloistered arch that led into the stacks. A staircase climbed directly to his right, its flanking walls decorated with maces and halberds and massive crossbows.

Charles Vandeleur, Archiviste Principal. A spidery arrow pointed into the recesses of the library.

Now why, Deacon suddenly thought, is the damned place lying wide open? Who left the door unlocked? He felt as if the archway might close upon him like the jaws of a shark. He shifted his revolver to his right hand and thumbed off the safety-catch.

"Monsieur?"

The word was like the inquiring mew of a cat.

"Monsieur, ici. Je suis ici."

The girl slipped shyly from the shadowed alcove.

She looked, Deacon thought, sweet enough to eat; blonde curls bobbed, blue eyes round with apprehension.

The lieutenant smiled reassuringly.

"Are you one of the soldiers who has been sent from England?" she asked in French.

"I am."

"To rescue the one named Paget?"

"Yes. Who are you?"

"I am a first cousin of Lisa Vandeleur."

Deacon relaxed. "Where is Paget?"

"Come," said Vivien Vandeleur. "I will take you to him."

Trustingly, Deacon followed her.

Charles Vandeleur sighed with relief when he heard the silly owlhoot that Guy Leconte poked through the trap in the floor of the belfry. His fat cheeks were rosy with exertion and sweat beaded his brow.

"The smoke?" said Chales Vandeleur, on all fours. "What does the smoke mean, Guy? Is it the English or the Germans?"

Puffing, Leconte struggled through the aperture, closed the trap and, also on all fours, rested.

"Well, tell me."

"It is English," said Leconte.

Vandeleur sat back on his haunches. "So, Lisa was correct and I was in error. They did not come by parachute. They came across country. How many?"

"God only knows," said Leconte.

"Have they not been contacted?"

Leconte too sat back, uncomfortably folding his short plump legs. Like Charles Vandeleur he had fought against the Germans twenty-two years ago. Unlike Vandeleur he had not kept his figure and was emphatically not fit to engage in gruelling physical activity. He was a radio operator, and a good one, but he had "lost" his radio, and was quite unqualified as a runner.

"No, but it is them without doubt," he answered, hand on his breast to calm his thumping heart. The climb up the iron ladder of the bell tower had sapped his stamina. "They set the Pelican on fire."

"Did they, indeed!" said Vandeleur.

"Not a moment too soon." Leconte explained what had been taking place in the town since the archivist had come "on duty" to the belfry the previous evening.

"It is serious," said Vandeleur when his friend had completed his account. "Poor Sylvie. She would tell the swine nothing, of course."

"She would die before she would talk, I expect."

"Has the house-to-house search begun?"

"Yes, but Ribbeck—did I tell you the bastard's last name?—the German general was obliged to delay things a little when the dear old Pelican burst into flames. He allowed the fire engine and our crew to put it out."

"How much damage was done?"

"Only the roof was burned."

"Not the wine cellar?"

"No."

"God be praised for that, Guy, eh?"

Leconte did not laugh, his usual good humor blighted by lack of sleep and deep concern over the fate of his wife and five children whom he had dispatched, ten days ago, to stay with his sister in Paris and from whom, in spite of repeated telephone calls, he had heard nothing. In that respect Charles Vandeleur was favored. His only loved one, Lisa, was here with him. If Leconte had known how difficult the guerilla war would be, he would not have promised the Vandeleurs to man the radio, would have gone with his family to Paris. His road-haulage business was ruined in any case. All he had left was his radio. It was hidden in the priest-hole in the catacombs under the library and would surely be discovered by the SS during the course of their search.

Vandeleur's arm on his shoulder did not lift Leconte's gloom.

Leconte said, "Lisa may not know of the English arrival. She sent me to tell you that Paget must be moved. She expects us to help. An impossible job, moving an injured man through the streets while the Bosch—"

"Nothing is impossible, my friend. We have kept Paget out of enemy hands so far, have we not? We will manage."

"Perhaps. Perhaps."

The tripod telescope, a relic of the last war, stood by the slatted opening on the belfry's west face. On the floor were six rockets and a flare gun. In addition, Vandeleur had brought along four stick grenades and a gas-operated 8 mm semi-automatic rifle, the Model 1917, a heavy brute that he had lugged through the last days of trench warfare.

"There is nothing to be gained by continuing the watch," Charles Vandeleur said. "Now that the raiders have arrived, Lisa must be freed of the burden of moving Paget. She must be given time to make contact with the English. We will find a safe place for the scientist."

"Charles—" Leconte began, then thought better of his protest. "Of course, that is what we must do."

"Where will we take him?"

"To the station, perhaps. Georges is hidden there."

"Disguised as a porter," said Vandeleur. "The library—"

"No, no. Whoever gave the Germans our names will have exposed the library too. We dare not go there."

"But the radio—?"

"The contact is broken, Charles."

"Can't you find a short-wave set to relay a message to London through Paris or Dunkirk?"

"Impossible," said Leconte. "The operation is already rolling.

Why do we need to contact London? If the Bosch pick up the message they won't rest until it is traced."

"Are they so well equipped?"

"They could go to the moon and conquer it with such equipment."

Vandeleur lifted the semi-automatic. "Shall we take my old St. Etienne and some of these mashers," he stuck three grenades into his belt, "to help us on our way? It may come to a fight yet, old friend, if the British are here in numbers."

"I'll take the flares."

"No need. You have enough to carry as it is." Charles Vandeleur affectionately patted his comrade's paunch. "I will be glad to get out of here. Hard boards are sore on ancient bones."

"After you," Leconte said.

The couple descended the ladder to the base of the bell tower. Vandeleur opened the door and peeped into the street. A square of grass surrounded the church, no trees. The street appeared to be empty.

"You see? Luck is with us, Guy."

"Go then—but not too fast."

The Frenchmen hurried down the little path and through the gate into the street. In muted morning light the fine old houses seemed to lean in on them.

There was something almost farcical in the sight of two respectable middle-aged men behaving so stealthily in the setting of the provincial town. Minutes away was Guy Leconte's house, a ghost house now, servants dismissed, shutters nailed, the garden growing weedy.

Everything was so familiar, so cosy, so friendly, that Charles and Guy might have been stealing home from a late-night carouse in the club of the Societé des Amis—except that they were perfectly sober and death, not sleep, awaited them round the corner.

"Not so quickly, please, Charles," puffed Guy Leconte.

Vandeleur slowed. He glanced back along the street, back past church and tower to the curve where the Rue Picarde swung sedately out of the so-called "business quarter." Winter and summer he walked by that route to the library, sometimes in company with Lisa, more often alone. He had experienced all seasons and weathers here and found contentment.

Danger and death were memories to which he had neglected to pay proper homage. The Frenchmen rounded the corner of the Rue Picarde and the Avenue de Champagne.

Fat Guy Leconte saw the Germans first.

The house-search patrol was composed of eight SS soldiers under the command of a sergeant, backed by a two-man light-machine-gun crew in the back of an Adler wagon. Two old sisters, named Vanderveen, had been winkled from their home. To the amusement of the soldiers, they were making a great fuss, swearing and stamping while the Germans teased them with bayonets. The car, engine running, had drawn abreast of the knot on the pavement.

"Get back, get back," Guy Leconte hissed, thrusting himself against Vandeleur.

Too late.

"Halt. Halt. Halt or we will shoot you."

Charles Vandeleur had halted for nobody when he was twenty-eight, and had outrun many German bullets. Why should things be different now that he was fifty?

Turning, he stumbled back around the corner into the Rue Picarde. Guy Leconte lurched behind him. As he ran, Charles Vandeleur worked the mechanism of the St. Etienne, ramming the stiff, disused locking bolt against the magazine.

"Cover, take cover, Guy," he cried.

They had made no distance on the corner, no distance at all. They seemed to be running fast but covering no ground, as if the pavement had become a conveyor belt that slid away beneath their feet. The wrought-iron gate of the Delbos house was the only shelter they could find, just twenty yards from the corner.

Vandeleur flung himself behind the gate post. Leconte, staggering past him, his hand to his chest, breath sawing in his fat throat, plunged up the path and fell heavily into a border flowerbed.

Through the trembling leaves of a linden tree, Charles Vandeleur glimpsed the movement of the Adler wagon, the gray dart of uniforms. The SS were running almost as fast as the car could travel, boots reverberating on the pavement, voices loud in the still morning air. There was no barrage, no whine and blast of shells as there had been last time he had faced the Bosch with a gun in his hand. He was down on one knee and his back ached and the St. Etienne felt very, very heavy in his hands.

"Run, Guy, for the house," he shouted.

He knew that Guy could fight no more. Retreat was all that was left to him. He thanked God that he had not allowed himself to grow fat with comfortable living and had worked on the tennis court whenever time allowed and with the boxing bag in the hall of his house.

The Adler wagon came wide, squealing.

Vandeleur saw the machine gun swivel. In reflex, he fired a hot, shuddering burst from the St. Etienne.

First blood to me! Hah!

But nothing happened.

The Adler whizzed past and the soldiers did not come around the corner into his field of fire. Fast, but not rash. Yes. Young but not impetuous. Yes. Disciplined, yes, and trained in fighting, yes, in the nature of the new war which had carried combat into the quiet streets of this bourgeois town.

Vandeleur selfishly wished that Lisa could see him now, see what the old archivist was made of.

Of Philip Paget, the cause of it, Vandeleur did not think at all.

What he was doing, what he would do, were part of the bridge between his past and his future. His past was a French war against the Germans. His future was Lisa and all the grandchildren he would never see.

He fought for them.

Let me kill enough of the Bosch to make my sacrifice worthwhile. Please, God, let me do that much.

The gun was hot in his hands, and felt lighter.

The Bosch would come over the wall in the shelter of the linden tree. A pair would be left at the corner, two more sent to infiltrate the garden of the Baum's house. Opposite was a high fence— Monsieur de Pertat's rose bushes flourished behind it—which gave protection from a frontal assault. He dared not change position or seek better cover in the house. The truth was that he did not want to. He had a solid stone pillar to lean on, the automatic rifle and, yes, four grenades.

The motorwagon; he wanted to destroy the motorwagon.

Behind him Guy emitted a gagging shout. Charles would have swung in response to the sound except that, at that moment, the Adler came again, roaring close against the pavement's edge. The gunner squatted like a toad in the back, the machine gun chattering. Bullets spanged about Charles Vandeleur's head. He replied, the St. Etienne clutched in his hands, tight but not choked. Stone chips sprayed him. A fleck of paint from the gate smarted in his left eye. Then the motorwagon was gone, squealing, and he heard shouts.

Father in Heaven, are they calling on me to give myself up? Did they suppose he was a feeble old woman, like the Vanderveen sisters? He tucked the stock of the St. Etienne against his hip and fumbled the grenades from his belt.

"Show yourself with your hands in the air. We will not shoot you. We are not butchers. Show yourself. Come out and all will be well."

It was almost over, Charles Vandeleur instinctively realized.

It did not unduly surprise him when Guy spoke. He turned his head. Guy was seated in the center of the path, legs stuck out. He resembled a gigantic baby. He had been shot through the center of the chest. His arms lay slack, fists curled. He wore an expression of abject apology.

"Ch—Ch—friend."

The face pinched. Leconte's mouth opened. He shrugged. It was not an expression in the French style, but death snatching at him. Blood came out of his open mouth. Suddenly he tumbled on to his back.

Yes, thought Charles Vandeleur, I suppose it's best to do it alone. He screwed the cap from a stick grenade, jerked the bead vigorously, counted two and, rising, hurled the grenade towards the corner.

The German shout was swallowed up by the explosion. Leaves and granular dust billowed over Charles. Shrieks lingered after the din of the explosion had died. The guttural cries of the SS troops rose in pitch. Yes, they too are afraid now. Angry, probably, but also afraid. Reaching back, Charles found Leconte's ankle and patted it. Then he had no more time, not if he wanted the motorwagon.

When the wagon came again, machine gun blazing, Charles Vandeleur was ready for it. He rose from his knees and ran forward, flung two grenades underarm at very short range and, sawn in half by a stream of bullets, pitched and slid to the pavement. He hung on, though, saw the wagon hurtle on, machine gun chattering, swivelling as the gunner scrambled to his feet. And the wagon vanished. And there were five dead Germans in the Rue Picarde, a fair sum to pay, Charles Vandeleur might have reckoned, for the lives of two old Frogs who had all but outlived their usefulness.

"Where are you taking me?" Deacon asked.

"To Lisa. By a safe route."

"Into the street?" Deacon hesitated.

"It is a—a courtyard. Quite safe."

Yielding, Deacon allowed her to draw on.

The corridor was in darkness. In niches the marble busts of famous soldiers scowled obscurely at him. The corridor ended in a glass-panelled door. The girl led him through it. The smell was reminiscent of Trinity again, only older, as if the dust had not stirred in this part of the library for many years. Sounds were muffled. The girl's fingers were cold.

She gripped Deacon's hand tightly. Though they were still at ground level the atmosphere was of a catacomb deep under the earth. Light filtered from narrow slits by the curved roof. This portion of the library was the medieval heart of the building.

As if to confirm it, the girl paused at the corridor's end where a tiny door pierced a wall constructed of massive stone blocks; the *scriptorum* of the seventh-century Abbey of St. Félice. Lisa had described it to him. He remembered now. The monument was famous.

"What is this place?" he asked.

"The library, monsieur."

"Is it not the *scriptorum*?"

"*Pardon?*"

"It does not matter," Deacon said softly.

Unsure of her direction the girl finally turned right.

The couple followed the post-Roman wall for ten or a dozen

paces, along a corridor patently built in the nineteenth, not the seventh, century. A door admitted them to a well-lighted room divided into study cubicles, each with a desk and chair. Books lined the walls. An assistant's cubby was crowded with filing cabinets.

The girl steered Deacon through the reading-room and into a main corridor, turned left and, still clutching Deacon's hand, pulled him on towards a studded door at the end of a vaulted chamber.

The door was unlocked.

The girl asked Deacon to open it.

Deacon released her hand, put his hand to the handle, a crook of iron as large as a flintlock, and pushed. Well-oiled and easy, the weight of the door rested in Deacon's fingers. Daylight streamed through the jamb.

"Go on, monsieur."

"Where does this lead?"

"I told you, it is safe."

She sounded like a spoiled brat, denied her own way.

"Go through, go through," she urged.

"Not," said Deacon, "just yet."

She gave him a nudge with her shoulder, plump breasts pressing against his arm. Deacon snared her forearm, the Webley held so that the barrel was pointed into Vivien's face.

"In England, ma'm'selle," the lieutenant said, "we are very polite." He hugged her, left hand under her breasts. Fitting her backside against his thighs, he hauled her against his chest. "Ladies first."

Deacon kicked the door. It swung ponderously open, flooding the corridor with light.

The girl screamed.

She thrashed against him but Deacon held her very tightly and, using her shoulder as a brace, stiffened his wrist, aimed and fired two shots at the machine gun which had been set up twenty yards in front of the doorway.

The Germans were caught unawares but gave away no targets. They had not, however, anticipated gunfire. Orders were forgotten.

Involuntarily the SS corporal squeezed the MG's trigger.

Deacon thrust the girl forward and flung himself to the left. The burst was short but quite sufficient to kill Mademoiselle Vivien Vandeleur instantly.

Deacon did not see her fall. He was already haring back along the corridor in search of escape.

An *al fresco* luncheon, prepared by company cooks from food-stuffs scrounged from local hotels, was carried to the office of the Clerk of Works. An office table, spread with a linen cloth, was set with steaming dishes and a dozen bottles of fine French wine.

The Obergruppenführer scooped *mushrooms à la princesse*, grilled sweetbreads, peas, asparagus and several thick slices of roast lamb casually on to his plate. Staudt, who had not eaten since 4 a.m., was more appreciative. He poured wine for the general and carried the glass to the table where Ribbeck, between mouthfuls, raged about a situation which, as it happened, was about to deteriorate even further.

Sturmbannführer Staudt mananged only a few morsels before the first interruption occurred.

SS Hauptsturmführer Wester apologetically brought news that the "missing" motorcycle unit had been found dead by the blown bridge at the Quern canal. Ribbeck buried the tines of his dinner-fork into the table top and stamped and strutted about the office.

Staudt questioned the Haupsturmführer and extracted all the information necessary to draw the conclusion that a British raiding party had somehow penetrated the town's defences. The incident with the flags and the arson at the Pelican Inn had not, after all, been the work of a French zealot.

While the Obergruppenführer vented his spleen on the hapless Wester, the major managed to do some sort of justice to the lamb. He was careful to make necessary responses to the general's rhetorical questions. An efficient company commander, Wester had already arranged for a party to bring in the corpses and the remaining BMW machines and had sent two light tanks up to Quern to check any further penetration.

Hardly had Wester gone, however, than the OC of 18th

Company, Hans Mauseberg, delivered two other items of information which, taken in context, disturbed Staudt almost as much as they enraged the general.

A routine patrol in the Avenue de Champagne had been attacked by two armed Frenchmen and four soldiers were killed. The Frenchmen had, of course, been shot. They were soon identified as Guy Leconte and Charles Vandeleur.

"What were they doing in the Avenue de Champagne?" Ribbeck demanded.

"As far as I can make out, Herr General," Mauseberg answered, "they were walking."

"But they were armed, were they not?"

"With an old semi-automatic rifle and half a dozen grenades."

"I want every house in that area searched."

"It is being done, Herr General."

"Searched from chimney to cellar."

"Yes, sir."

"Where are the bodies?"

"I had them taken to the undertaker's shop."

"Bring them out, Mauseberg. Place them on a flatbed truck and drive it slowly around the square."

"Herr General?"

"Do as I say."

"Sir."

"You have other news?"

Mauseberg clicked his heels and took refuge in formality as he delivered an account of the shooting at the library.

"Where is the English soldier now?" said Ribbeck.

"He—it appears that he escaped, sir."

"How could he escape? Was the library not under guard?"

"He—he escaped through a lavatory window, Herr General."

"Through a lavatory window? God in Heaven! And ascended a ladder made of rope and vanished, I suppose?"

"We have two units in close pursuit, Herr General. He will be caught."

"Take him alive," said Ribbeck. "On no account must he be 'accidentally' shot. Do you understand me, Hauptsturmführer?"

"Yes, sir."

"Keep me informed of your progress."

"Sir."

Mauseberg clicked his heels and departed on the double.

Though he gave every appearance of being calm, Staudt recognized the general's sanguinity in the crushing set of the jaw and the steel-hard glint in his eye.

"I am sure that the raider will soon be captured, sir," Staudt said.

"I am sure of nothing," Ribbeck said, "except that the SS Totenkopf has sacrificed ten trained soldiers and gained not one inch of ground or one life in return."

"When we lay hands on the English scientist—" Staudt began, but the general cut him off.

"Damn the English scientist! We are at war, Staudt. It is not a game of boy scouting though that is how it may seem to the British. How many prisoners are at this farm?"

"Eighteen."

"I wish to see them."

"May I ask why, Herr General?"

"They must know something."

"They were all questioned, sir."

"Not with enough conviction, Staudt. When one or two are shot, the others will talk."

"Herr General, what can they tell us?"

"It is what they will tell their compatriots. Do you want another fire, another flag-burning, Staudt? Do you want us to appear weak and foolish to that rabble in the square? I will show them what we are made of. I will show them what the soldiers of the Reich do to its enemies."

"Do you wish me to bring the prisoners here, sir?"

"I will fetch them myself," said Ribbeck.

"And my orders, Herr General?"

"Bring out the tanks, Sturmbannführer." Ribbeck lifted his greatcoat and hat from the chair.

"The tanks?"

"All the artillery," said Ribbeck. "Ring the square."

"Why, sir?"

"If these French peasants will not talk," said Obergruppen-führer Ribbeck, "then they will die. Die on the end of our guns."

"It would be a—a massacre, Herr General."

"It will be a lesson, Staudt, one they will not easily forget."

"Nope," Buz Campbell said, "I'm not hanging around waiting to be taken out of here and shot."

"They wouldn't dare," said the pilot officer.

"But yes, I believe they would," said the Mayor.

"Aye, man, it's a better bet than gettin' shipped off t'Germany," said the Geordie. "I'm siding with the sergeant."

"What's yer plan?" asked the AC private.

"First I've got to persuade them to open the door again," said Buz Campbell. "When that's done, we'll need weapons."

"But there are no weapons," said the pilot officer. "Not even a blessed hayfork."

"The krauts have weapons," said Buz.

"This plan stinks, if you ask me," said the private.

Buz paused. He had no choice but to trust them. "There will be covering fire."

"Come again, sarge?"

"You heard me."

Guizot, the Mayor, smiled. "Ah! You are not alone?"

"Right," said Buz.

"Bloody 'ell."

"How many, sarge?"

"Enough," Buz answered.

"What do we do once the door's open?"

"Keep down and get ready to run for it," said Buz. "Once you're outside, it's every man for himself."

"Maybe we should stick together," suggested the private.

"Suit yourselves," said Buz. "I reckon you should head for the Quern road with all the artillery you can find. Be ready to fight your way through a road-block, though, a mile and a half out."

"Where's the Quern road?" asked the Geordie.

"Mr. Mayor, will one of your compatriots volunteer to go with them?" said Buz.

"I will go personally," said Guizot.

"No, I can use you in town," said Buz.

"In that case, perhaps Perrinot will agree to act as navigator."

"Ask him," said Buz. "And spread word what's happening. Anybody who's too yellow to make a break for it had better get out of range at the back of this place and stay there."

"You, I take it," said the pilot officer, "will be the first man through the door?"

"Who else?" said Buz Campbell.

"When do we go?" asked the infantry man.

"Right now," Buz answered.

Deacon stepped through the lavatory window into a narrow alley on the north-east side of the library. After sprinting through the maze-like interior of the building he had temporarily lost his sense of direction. The alley gave him no clue; a mossy gable rose directly before him, topped by a steep slate roof. To the right there was only another gable, windowless and dank; left, the protrusion of a railed step screened an opening to the street.

Deacon chose the back route towards the gable. If he guessed wrong and it turned out to be a cul-de-sac, he was in serious trouble. The SS would be in the process of flinging a net over the library. Without doubt there would be troops in the street by now. He ran to the blind corner, poked his head around it, found one exit blocked by a wall. The other offered an unpromising extension of an alley. Devil's choice, Deacon, old man. He headed down the alley. It was hardly wider than his shoulders and smelled of horse dung and rotting straw. It led him to another intersection. This time there was no choice. Soldiers, running down the lane, had already spotted him.

The stable had been partly converted into a garage. A single dirty petrol pump stood like a sentinel before padlocked wooden doors. Inset into the large doors, however, was a smaller door, locked too. Deacon put the Webley into the keyhole and fired two shots. He rammed the little door with his shoulder and catapulted into an empty room with a concrete floor and a glass roof. The stench of horses and gasoline was strong. Pools of grease stained the floor. A car inspection pit and four horse stalls. Another set of wooden doors on the west wall obviously led out to the street.

Deacon clambered up on the nearest stall, slung an elbow around the wooden pillar and, stretching, hammered the butt of the

Webley against the whorled pane overhead. He swung himself to one side as glass rained down. He reached up again, tapped away the jagged edges, stuck the gun in his tunic and levered himself up through the hole. Below, the clatter of the door indicated that the SS were hot on his heels.

The vee of the roof ridge was uninviting.

Deacon straddled the glass and looked frantically behind him. Even as he spotted the iron ladder, glass disintegrated, spurting upwards, sprayed by bullets. Deacon swung himself on to the ladder, clambered up it and bellied himself on to a steep slate roof. The chimney stack and a boarded walkway seemed very far away.

Army boots were clumsy to climb in. Deacon worked himself up with knees and fingers. It was eighteen months since he had last climbed rock but his arms had lost little of their strength. He tried not to panic, in spite of the shouts that echoed up from the garage. Reaching the chimney he swept his arm about it, tugged out his revolver and twisted around. A split second longer and it would have been too late. The German's expression was querulous, the helmeted head perched on the rim of the roof. Deacon squeezed the trigger twice. The head vanished as the soldier fell dead through the remains of the glass roof.

Heaving himself up, Deacon got his body behind the stack and, fumbling, found ammo for the Webley. Protected by the chimney, he reloaded.

Two helmeted heads: Deacon aimed and fired, pushed himself from the stack on to the boardwalk that spindled along the crest of the roof. He danced along it and stepped down on to a flat, macadamized roof.

Big air ventilators hunched at regular intervals and a high edge protected him from the street. The tall gable of the library seemed far off. There was no immediate sign of pursuit, though the Germans would surely be ringing the block. Deacon had no intention of being trapped on the rooftops.

No longer did it seem possible, however, to pull off the impossible mission. He had lost contact with Campbell and McNair and, targeted by the Germans, could not risk making contact with Lisa, even if he knew where to find her. The best he could hope for now was to evade the SS, hide out until dark and, somehow, make his way back across country to the coast. What was more, he must do it entirely without aid. After his experience with the blonde girl, he could trust nobody in this town.

Moving rapidly, the lieutenant crossed the flat roof, climbed another sweep's ladder and surveyed the scene from the upper rungs. The Boulevard Sainte Barbe was on one side, a nondescript road on the other. On the boulevard the soldiers were marshalling and Deacon did not tarry long enough to give them sight of him.

He lowered himself down the shallow slope towards the road which promised shelter in shops and workshops. Drainpipes dropped from the roof's edge, old and rusted. Deacon was in no position to be fussy. He skirted the edge of the roof, walking upright, and stepped down on to the top of the second-last house in the block, lowered himself over the edge of the roof and draped the length of his body over the upper floor of shops.

A curtained window, a solid stone sill, closed wooden shutters carved with fleur-de-lys, the bolts for an awning, an earth-filled window-box cradled on iron stanchions; the wall was a climber's dream. Deacon picked his way from hold to hold with speed and assurance, dropping the last twelve feet to a pavement. Just as he hit the deck, however, an armored car swept round the curve from the square. Deacon lunged backwards, still reeling from the drop, into the doorway of the cobbler's workshop. He did not know if he had been seen but had no doubt at all that sharp-eyed soldiers in the armored car would spot him quickly enough as they passed. He drew the Webley and held it in a firing position, left hand clasped round right wrist, legs spread.

Behind him the wooden door clicked open and a gnarled hand caught his shoulder.

"This way, sir, this way," said the old man in French in a hoarse whisper.

Deacon stepped inside.

The old man closed the door.

Deacon slanted the revolver and held it to the man's throat.

The face was as gnarled and pallid as the hand. A leather beret covered wispy gray hair. The eyes were foxy, the color of paraffin, the mouth stretched in a smile that showed three tobacco-blackened teeth.

"This way, this way." The old cobbler tugged urgently at his sleeve, but Deacon would not be caught again. "This way. Quick. Quick."

The workshop was cramped, the floor ankle-deep in shrivelled clips of leather and wood shavings. There was almost no light, the window being covered by a cracked, green linen blind.

The old man and the English lieutenant stared at each other while the armored car growled past, followed immediately by another heavy vehicle, possibly a tank.

The old man nodded as if to answer Deacon's upspoken question. "Arras, the Somme, the Marne, the second battle of Verdun." He dabbed a crooked finger into the breast of his leather apron. "I fought there with you Tommies. Fifty, I was, and a volunteer. I told a lie about my age, see. I shod horses and made leathers until there were no more Frenchmen left for to fight. Then I fought, sir. Verdun, the Somme, Arras; at Soissons on August the second. See the leg."

The old man pointed downward proudly and Deacon saw that his left foot was made of painted wood.

"I understand." Deacon lowered his revolver. "But why are you still here? The Germans cleared the town."

"Germans! *Phaap!*" The cobbler spat into the shavings. "I hide here. My wife, my daughters, my grandchildren. We hide here." He rapped the wooden foot upon the floorboards and scraped away shavings to reveal a small trap with a rope handle. "Down there. You hide with us too?"

"How did you spot me?"

"Luck, only luck, sir. I was spying, see, when you fell from my roof," said the cobbler. "Hide. It will be safe. I even have a cupboard down below. I put you in the cupboard. If the Germans find us, we give ourselves up and tell them nothing about you in the cupboard. After dark—you leave."

Deacon put his hand on the old man's beret and skimmed it over the paraffin-colored eyes. "Old soldier, I thank you, but I can't wait. I have to get out immediately. Besides, I'm not alone."

"You are here for the English parachutist, no?"

"Now how the devil did you know about him?"

"My nephew's eldest boy, Georges, he looks after your English comrade."

"Where?"

The cobbler shrugged. "It is better not to ask. Georges tells me, though, when he comes two days ago to borrow my daughter's husband's uniform. My daughter's husband is fighting now."

"Uniform?"

"Railway porter. It is a disguise, see. Georges is a horse-doctor, a veterinarian, but he is a good Frenchman who does not go south with the horses. He stays here to fight the Germans."

"Does Georges know where the English parachutist is hidden?"

"But of course. He gives him medical attention, two times each day."

"And the railway station, where Georges hides out?"

"One minute away."

"Will you take me there?"

"It would be easier after dark."

"I can't wait that long. It has to be now."

"I understand, sir. I will take you there at once."

"My God!" said Deacon. "What a small world it is."

"In St. Félice," said the cobbler, "the world is smaller than anywhere else. Come now, sir. We will find our way through my timber shed to the road in front of the *gare*."

P.B. was disappointed that there were no German vehicles in the farmyard, only a raddled old Renault lorry with a buckled wheel which had been shoved into a cowshed at the back of the barn. A rooster perched on top of the cab. Hen-shit smeared the windscreen. The slats of the flatbed were broken, the bed strewn with rotting straw. A sniff at the gas cap told P.B. there was some juice in the tank, though, and maybe the wheel would hold up long enough to carry them far enough along the road to pick up another truck.

He didn't hang around in the cowshed. It was too close for comfort to the kitchen door. Anyhow, Buz might decide to make a break at any minute and if he wasn't in position to back the sarge, it would be a massacre. He went round the back of the barn slid over the dyke and crawled to the place where he'd stashed the

Bren. The spot gave him a wide field of fire. He glanced up at the wine bottle on the pole and wished it was full again. His mouth was as dry as a camel's crotch. He settled down behind the iron trough in the weeds and waited.

In thirty minutes, if Buz hadn't made a move, he would.

It turned out to be nothing like thirty minutes, more like three.

Shouting started up again. Not just old Buz giving it big licks, a chorus of male voices all ranting and raving. Startled, the guards backed off. They hiked up their carbines. One of them yelled across the yard. Half a dozen krauts came out of the kitchen, followed by the SS captain. They were all within range.

Christ, P.B. thought, the massacre's on the other foot now, okay.

P.B. had hand-filled four magazines, twenty-six rounds to each, from a collection of loose chargers he had acquired over the last few days. He set the Bren's trigger for continuous fire. Sixty round per minute, normal rate, would give him a half-minute burst from each magazine, near enough. No chance the barrel would burn up on him. He hadn't lugged the 23 lb. brute around all bloody morning just to have it conk out on him now. He would make every bullet count. Sliding on his belly, P.B. locked the bipod in vertical. He would hoist the gun forward and rest the bipod on a brick abutment by the galvanized trough. From the position he would have a traverse of 42°, just the right elevation to chop the krauts in half.

Krauts were streaming out of the farmhouse. Hopping mad at the ruckus, the captain jabbered in German. Some of the krauts had been feeding their faces. They were still chewing and buttoning themselves into their uniforms. They looked like any army guard rousted out on short notice.

Pushing the Bren before him, P.B. inched forward. He was pumped up again. He wanted to laugh, yell, draw the bastards' attention so he could see their faces when he blasted them.

Eight carbines and two automatic rifles. Same as before. A slice of the yard protected by the big dung cart was the only piece P.B.'s Bren couldn't reach. But he could reach it easy with the Lee Enfield by shifting fifteen or twenty feet right. He doubted if the krauts would be standing still. The German captain wasn't mucking about. Maybe he didn't like having his dinner inter-rupted. Vaguely P.B. speculated on what might be stashed in the farmhouse. What sort of grub had the krauts found? Was there booze?

Through the weeds, P.B. watched a corporal plaster himself against the side of the barn. He crept along and, with the butt of his carbine, battered the locking bar. The soldiers were tense. P.B. suspected that they had been ordered to shoot on sight anybody who came out of the hole. No names, no fucking pack drill. The captain knew Buz was up to something. He would take no chances. The bar swung up. The barn door swung open a wee bit. Nobody galloped out. Buz wasn't daft. He had the captain taped. The captain shouted angrily. No reply from the barn. Shouting went on. Any sensible British officer would have walked away. But krauts were used to being obeyed.

P.B. McNair recognized an order to fire.

The German's salvo was deafening. It sent pigeons up from the cobbles, swallows zooming from the eaves. Even the rooks across the fields were startled enough to take wing. With twenty or thirty rounds slammed into it, the barn door closed then swung open again, creaking in the silence.

The shouting had ceased.

Suddenly a hay bale came crashing out of the barn. It thudded against the door, which flew all the way open, and skidded out into the yard, drawing a hail of German bullets.

P.B. McNair thought: Aye, that's a sign okay.

He shifted the Bren forward, slammed the tripod on the bricks, his elbows on the ground, planted butt to shoulder—and let her rip.

It was all over, near enough, in twenty seconds.

The cough of the Bren was lost in kraut gunfire.

The captain was the first to be blown away. Right where he stood. On the Bren's second sweep, six SS guards went with their officer to Kingdom Come. P.B. picked off two runners. A third kid was daft enough to fling himself against the barn wall. Two bullets took care of him. By the time the Bren's magazine was finished, there wasn't an upright German in the yard.

P.B. discarded the Bren, grabbed the Lee Enfield, hopped over the fence and flung himself into the vegetable patch. From there he got one of the runners who had doubled towards the kitchen. A quick tally of bodies sprawled about the yard told P.B. that he had disposed of eleven Germans. Braced on one knee he systematically pumped shots into those who were still moving. Then he rolled and scuttled into a caul of bushes in case one of the few krauts who had escaped was stupid enough to take a pot at him.

Three hay bales were walking out of the barn, each with four legs. P.B. laughed. The leading bale stopped by a German corpse and Buz scowled over the top of it. The guy beside him was an RAF officer.

"How's it going, wee man?" Buz shouted.

"No' bad," P.B. answered.

"Where are the rest of them?"

"Scarpered."

Cautiously Buz got to his feet. He signalled. Prisoners came nervously out of the barn. P.B. stayed put while two British soldiers and the RAF guy armed themselves. They were still no signs of the three krauts who had escaped. They would be legging it for town by now.

P.B. came forward.

"Where's Deacon?" Buz Campbell said.

"In town."

"How'd you find me?"

"Followed the lorry."

"Can we get out of here?"

"Aye. There's a farm truck round the corner."

"Show me."

P.B. led the sergeant round the barn into the cowshed, followed by the herd of prisoners who seemed to be attached to Buz by a string. They crowded into the cowshed and ringed the Renault.

Buz said, "Well. let's hope this baby goes."

"Listen, sergeant," said the RAF officer, "you're not going to abandon us, are you?"

"I've got things to do in town." Buz opened the cab door in search of the bonnet catch. He found it, jerked, and the tinny bonnet clanged. "If this thing moves, we'll run you into town."

"Town? Is that a good idea, man?" asked the Geordie.

"Nope," said Buz. "The best idea is for the three of you to find yourself guns and food, pack up and get the hell out of here into the countryside heading for Quern."

"Don't you need our help?" asked the RAF officer.

"From what I've seen in St. Félice," said Buz, as he walked to the front of the truck "it's going to be hard enough for two of us to get in there. None of you know your way around the burg?"

None of the Britishers did.

Buz nodded. "Right. Go see what you can scrounge. Keep together and keep your eyes peeled. The krauts may still be around, though my guess is they've lit out for the hills."

"To report, of course?" said the pilot officer.

"It's a mile, anyway, to the nearest German unit, I reckon," said Buz from under the Renault's bonnet. "That'll give us a quarter of an hour before we can expect trouble."

"It isn't much of a start, sarge."

"So why waste it hangin' round here?" said Buz.

"Monsieur, what is it you must do in St. Félice?" asked one fat Frenchman.

P.B. saw Buz hesitate. He wouldn't have trusted no Frog, especially a sleek one.

Buz said, "Do you know somebody called Vandeleur?"

"Of course. He is our archivist. In the library. We have a famous library here, you know."

"Can you get in touch with Vandeleur, or his daughter?"

The Frenchman nodded.

"Hey, Buz?" P.B. said.

"What?"

"Think I'll take a wee walk."

"Right. Bring guns."

"Right."

Deflated after the heat of the action, P.B. went out into the farmyard to search for weapons and drinkable alcohol, not necessarily in that order.

Two or three minutes later he heard the Renault's engine whine and splutter reluctantly to life. When he came out of the farmhouse laden with loot, the lorry was shuddering by the corner of the barn. Most of the prisoners had departed, including the Brits. Two old Frogs were standing in the back of the flatbed, hanging on to the slats for dear life. The fat Frenchman, Mayor of St. Félice, was in the cab with Buz.

"Hop aboard, wee man."

P.B. hoisted his sacks into the cab, stowed the guns he had found into the footwell and squeezed against the Frenchman. He had left the Bren behind. Where they were going he didn't imagine they would have much chance to set it up. Besides, he was tired of lugging it around and the gun had served its purpose.

The lorry's windscreen was smeared with chicken-shit. Buz crouched to see through it as he steered the vehicle around the yard and out along the road by which he had entered Melampyre.

Glancing from the side window, P.B. caught a glimpse of the three Britishers traversing a field, heading south-west.

"You got rid of them?"

"Yeah," said Buz. "I figure they'll do better on their own. If they're lucky, they might connect with an Allied outfit some place out there."

"But we're goin' back for Deacon?"

"This guy, Monsieur Guizot, says he can find the Vandeleurs. We'll wait while he goes into town."

P.B. said nothing. He couldn't understand why Buz would want to pursue Deacon. It wasn't anything they should have been involved in in the first place. He lifted one of the German field-packs on to his lap. Two full bottles of schnapps clinked cheerfully against the hand-guns.

The Renault wobbled out of the farmyard into a narrow, tree-lined lane.

P.B. felt sleepy.

They travelled only a mile before the Renault's tank ran dry. The lorry was still moving, though, when the Frenchman, Guizot, pointed to a hiding-place. Christ knows, it wasn't much. Trees and bushes swept over a field entrance and at least they would be hidden from the road. Buz cranked the wheel. The Renault lurched into the leafy cave and stopped.

Guizot opened the door.

"There is no word to thank you, monsieur."

"Just come back with the information," Buz said. "That'll be thanks enough, Mr. Mayor."

"I give my promise."

With the two old Frogs in tow, the Mayor of St. Félice set off on foot across the flat pasture towards the back of a row of villa-style houses.

Suddenly it was deathly quiet. The engine hissed, cooling. A fly buzzed the inside of the windscreen. P.B. unbuckled the field-pack and brought out the schnapps.

"Want some, Buz?"

"Sure. One slug can't do us any harm."

P.B. uncorked the bottle and handed it to the Canadian who tilted the neck to his mouth and drank. He gasped, shook his head and handed the bottle back to P.B. P.B. drank too.

Buz Campbell's smile was crimped. He leaned his forearms on the steering wheel and peered through the chicken-shit into the leaves.

"Know what they call this, wee man?"

"Aye?"

"What then?"

"Do or fuckin' die," said P.B. McNair.

"Lisa?"

"Who is it? Jeff, is it you?"

"Yeah. At last."

"Come down, quickly."

Deacon descended the ladder into the corn pit.

She was not quite the same untainted young girl that he had known in Quern before the war but, in spite of her anxiety and obvious exhaustion, she was just as beautiful. It cost Deacon an effort of will not to take her in his arms. He sensed that she was embarrassed by their former relationship, the fact that they had been lovers.

"How did you find us?"

"It's a long story, which will keep," said Deacon.

The cobbler had led him to the railway station where the plump horse-doctor, disguised in a railway porter's uniform, was lying low. In turn Georges had conducted him to Paget's hiding-place. Deacon had accompanied Georges without a qualm. In better times he was the kind of Frenchman who, by sheer *joie de vivre*, would have won Deacon as a friend. Georges, however, was grieving for a girl, Sylvie, who had been shot by the SS. Hatred for the Germans, like the dark green uniform, sat ill upon such a jovial man.

"Where are the others?" asked Lisa.

"There aren't any others," said Deacon. "Apart from a couple of army types I picked up on the way who have, alas, been captured."

"Will they talk?"

"To the Germans? God, no!"

"Three, is that all? Major Holms told Guy, our radio operator, that a raiding party was being sent in?"

"How long ago did you receive the message?"

"At the same time as we were asked to look out for Paget. I told Guy to ask that you be one of them, so that I could be sure—if you understand."

"I started out in a tank," said Deacon, "but it didn't get far. The Totenkopf have the sector sewn up all the way along the high road to Quern. I suspect that Holms, like everybody else, under-estimated the pace of the Nazi thrust. Was there much fighting here?"

"No, only local resistance. St. Félice was occupied by the SS Leibstandarte. The Totenkopf took over only after Paget's plane was brought down. It seems that the Germans knew a great deal more than we did about your Mr. Paget. There is an informer."

"Your cousin," said Deacon, hesitantly, "a girl called Vivien—"

"We never did trust her. She has a German lover," put in Georges who was stooped over his patient at the far end of the pit.

"It makes no matter now. She's dead," said Deacon. "She tried to turn me over to the SS but—well—I managed to evade them. Your cousin caught bullets that were intended for me, I'm afraid."

"Good riddance!" said Georges.

Lisa said, "It does not surprise me. The entire operation with this man, with Paget, was a German trick. It was never Maurice Linhart's intention to fly back to England and help the Allies. Linhart is a Nazi sympathizer. The scientists in England, Paget included, were very gullible, Jeff, do you not think?"

"It's all Greek to me," said Deacon. "My instructions were simply to rendezvous with you and escort Paget to the beach at Bovet, near Dunkirk, where a navy vessel will be waiting. I imagine that plan's gone west too, though."

"Paget is important," said Lisa. "Too important to be permitted to fall into German hands."

Georges had lit a candle. By its light he was changing the dressings that surrounded the ugly plaster that coated Paget's thigh. The scientist thrashed and groaned. Georges crooned reassuringly as he worked.

"Radio," said Deacon. "Am I right? Isn't Paget an expert in radio defence systems?"

"Yes," said Lisa. "He is also very ill. His thigh is broken and he has a fever."

"The fever is down," said Georges.

"Can we move him?" asked Deacon.

"He cannot remain here," answered Georges. "Yes, with care, he may be moved."

"Is he sedated?"

"He has had about as much morphine as he can take for the time being," said Georges. "Besides, my supply is almost finished."

Craning his neck, Paget croaked. "Officer, officer? A word in your ear, officer."

"Is he delirious?" Deacon asked.

"Sometimes," answered Lisa. "When he is conscious, he is very afraid."

"One can hardly blame him," said Deacon. "Haven't the Germans searched the mill?"

"They came hurriedly at dusk yesterday, only two of them. They were not thorough," said Georges. "By chance both Lisa and I were here and I had given Paget an injection only minutes before so that he was deeply asleep and made no noise."

"Bit nerve-wracking, though," said Deacon.

"Officer, officer, here, here."

Deacon went over to the palliasse and knelt on the ground by Paget's side. "My name is Deacon. How are you feeling, old chap?"

"French, are you?"

"No, I'm English."

"You're young; too young."

"Actually, I'm pushing twenty-four."

Paget looked ghastly. His eyes were sunken in his skull and his skin had a yellowish tinge. A stark white plaster moulded the left thigh. Clotted cotton dressings covered stiching, stained with gentian. The odor of antiseptic, urine and sour sweat almost made Deacon gag.

"We have to carry water in," Lisa explained. "It is difficult to keep him clean."

"Of course," said Deacon.

"But I have done a reasonable job of repair," said Georges. "It is less difficult to set a human femur than a horse's bone. Provided the infection recedes, he should suffer no permanent injury."

"You're a British army officer?" Pager snatched at Deacon's sleeve.

"Quite right, old chap."

"Send them away. Send the French away."

"But they're friends. They've looked after you awfully well, you know."

"I have a secret. Send them away."

Deacon glanced at Lisa and Georges and shrugged apologetically. The couple retreated to the end of the pit by the iron ladder.

Tugging on Deacon's sleeve, Paget hoisted himself painfully from the bed. Deacon supported him.

"Closer," Paget whispered.

Obligingly Deacon inclined his head, offering his ear to Paget's mouth.

"I know what you think," Paget began, sibilantly. "You think I'm not right in the head."

"A little fevered, perhaps."

"Are you going to get me out of here?"

"I'm going to try."

"I can't walk."

"I'll find a truck, or something. Leave it to me, Dr. Paget."

"So you know who I am?"

"Of course. I was sent here by the British government to get you back to England. You're needed rather badly to help the war effort."

"Do you know why?"

"No," said Deacon. "Perhaps it's best that I don't."

"It was a trap all along. Linhart had no intention of returning to England. He had already been converted to Nazism. Lille was hell. Linhart wasn't even there. He'd gone. There were Germans. Waiting for me. Disguised Germans. Nicholson knew."

"Who's Nicholson?"

"My pilot. Nicholson was—he was a hero."

"Where's Nicholson now?"

"We flew out of Lille just as the Germans took the airfield. Minutes to spare. They had planes in the sky to chase us. Nicholson had been told to head for St. Félice, to avoid the guns or something. We were shot down. We didn't jump for it. He brought the plane down more or less in one piece. I was injured. The German patrols would have found me. Nicholson led them away."

"Perhaps he escaped?"

"They shot him. I saw them shoot him. I hid and did nothing."

"What could you do? You had a shattered thigh."

"The French came looking for me in the dark. How they found me I don't know. Perhaps Nicholson gave them a radio fix before we crash-landed. They came through the lines of the German soldiers to find me."

"But you don't trust them?" Deacon asked.

"Not after Linhart's trickery."

"Well, I'm here. The army's here. I'll get you home, never fear."

"You don't have to be so insufferably patronizing," Paget snarled. "I'm not a child. The truth is you may not be able to get me out of France at all. Am I not correct?"

"Absolutely," said Deacon. "The Germans have run the Allies almost to the sea. As you may have gathered, the SS are in total command of this town and are hunting high and low for you. Even so, I'm not without a certain resourcefulness. And I have friends to help me."

"French friends?"

"Good friends," said Deacon. "Think what they've done for you, old chap. They could have left you to die, couldn't they?"

"I suppose so," said Paget. "It isn't dying that bothers me. Look, officer, you must make me a promise. Swear that you won't let me fall into the hands of the Germans."

"It won't come to that."

Paget was quite rational now, anxious, fretful and afraid, but rational. He gripped Deacon's hand with surprising strength. "If it does, shoot me."

"I couldn't—"

"Don't be an idealistic young fool," said Paget. "All of this— the tricks, the planes, the dying—do you suppose it would have happened if it hadn't been for me? I'm *important* to the Germans. I know certain things. I can do certain things. Radionics. I can build a device—"

"Yes," Deacon interrupted. "You've made your point, Doctor Paget."

"Then promise. Swear you won't let them take me alive."

"Cheerfulness," said Deacon softly, "is only camouflage. It was never my intention to let the Germans take you alive. Believe me, if it comes to it, Doctor Paget, I'll shoot you without a moment's hesitation."

"Thank God!" Paget released the lieutenant's hand and sank back. Sweat slicked his face but he was relieved, vastly relieved. He said, "Nicholson would have done it, you know."

"Nicholson would also have had a damned good shot at getting you out, wouldn't he?"

"Yes. But how, how will you do it?"

"That's the rub, old chap," said Deacon. "Somehow I've got to find four wheels attached to a gas engine."

The black Mercedes sedan hove into view through the trees. It looked menacing even at a distance and before Campbell could make out the pennants and insignia of the general. It was travelling fast. Tire rumble deepened as the car left the suburban street and debouched on to the country road. Dust smoked behind it in an ochre cloud.

"Christ, what's that?" said P.B. McNair. "Is it yon Frog comin' back?"

"I doubt it," said Buz. "It's a kraut staff car."

"Lovely!" said P.B. McNair.

The soldiers were seated on a grass knoll, screened by bushes, at the mouth of the field track. They had been drinking moderately from the schnapps bottle and smoking cigarettes that P.B. had pilfered from dead Germans.

"Guns," Buz ordered. "Get the goddamn guns."

Lugers and rifles would not stop an armored sedan. Buz headed for the Renault. Switching on the engine, which spluttered and coughed weakly, he flung the stick into reverse and charged to the front of the truck.

P.B. was there for him.

"Shove! For Christ's sake, shove," Buz urged.

The engine caught for an instant, jerking the radiator away from the men. The wheels ground on the dry dirt track. P.B. and Buz flung themselves again upon the Renault, exerting every ounce of strength to maintain the vehicle's momentum.

Cresting the crown of the field track, the lorry picked up a little speed and trundled down to the roadway.

The Mercedes had no space to manoeuvre and the driver hadn't the wit to go with the braking swerve and allow the sedan to slew harmlessly off the road into the pasture and pass the hulk that had ponderously rolled into his path.

The Mercedes was doing close to forty miles per hour when it horned into the slats of the Renault truck.

The weight of the big sedan bulled the lightweight lorry on for fifteen or twenty yards then overturned it. The wreck halted, thrust against the banking by a stumpy willow, the Mercedes, almost undamaged, half-buried in the tangle, its engine howling and the young SS corporal slumped across its steering wheel.

P.B. dragged open the driver's door, hauled the corporal on to the road and kicked him on the side of the head. The corporal twitched. P.B. dragged him on to the banking out of harm's way.

Buz, meanwhile, introduced himself to the passenger.

"So, Herr General," said Buz, smiling fatly, "we meet again, right?"

Ribbeck was shaken by the crash and the suddenness with which the Britishers had appeared, but his agile brain grasped certain salient facts immediately.

Buz removed the Walther P38 from the Obergruppenführer's holster, checked the magazine to ensure that it was loaded, and tucked the Walther into his blouse. During that time the Luger, standard army issue, that he had redeemed from the captain at Melampyre never wavered from its aim on the general's carotid artery.

"Is my corporal dead?" said Ribbeck, in clumsy English.

"Nope, just sleeping," said Buz.

"Why don't you shoot me?" said Ribbeck.

"Not a hope, pal," said Buz.

"I will not cooperate with you."

"Goddamn right you will." Buz drew back from the passenger door to make way for P.B. McNair. "This is my buddy, General. He'll take care of you."

Ribbeck's eyes slithered in the direction of the second British soldier, a small monkey-like creature who would have been rejected on sight by recruiters of the SS Totenkopf and, indeed, by any reputable regiment in the Third Reich.

P.B. grinned and jabbed the kraut with the muzzle of the Lee Enfield, forcing him into the offside corner of the sedan. P.B. slid in beside him. A rifle was more useful than a German Luger—P.B. had one too—for he could stick the forward sight up the kraut's cavernous nostrils and rip his nose off if the bastard gave him any cheek. What he could not and would not do was kill the high brass. Bloody hell, Buz would have his arse for that. Without being told, P.B. knew that the SS Obergruppenführer was their passport to freedom.

At the front of the Mercedes, Buz pulled away shattered slats and debris. He got into the driver's seat and turned on the ignition. The engine roared hard and strong the moment Buz slung it into reverse. The Mercedes came away from the wrecked lorry. It dragged a torn wheel and a piece of French axle for ten yards then shed them and backed off down the country road clean as a whistle.

"Some baby," murmured Buz appreciatively.

"It will benefit you nothing to keep me prisoner," said Ribbeck through snake-thin lips, neither of the soldiers understood.

"A full tank too," said Buz. "How you doin', wee man?"

"Terrific!"

Buz fisted the wheel. He backed the Mercedes across the road, slotted the rear tires to the edge of the ditch and punched the stick into forward. He caught her as she surged eagerly, played power against the brake and, more gently, nosed her round to face back along the road into the suburbs and set off for the heart of St. Félice to find Second Lieutenant Jeffrey Deacon.

It seemed like pure luck that brought Deacon and Campbell together at the corn mill. Luck, like confusion, was one of the factors that nobody mentioned when they handed you the ticket to France. Partisans were few and not well organized. With Vandeleur and Leconte gone, their numbers had been reduced to a handful. None of the Vandeleurs' band, though, had been caught in the round-up and Pascal Fromont, the only one among them who knew where Paget was secreted, had been given SS Sturmbannführer Staudt's personal letter of clearance to enable him to escort his mother and his sister home.

Sheeted in a military shroud that Staudt had provided, Sylvie Fromont, made her last journey through the streets of St. Félice roped to a handcart.

"Allow me to furnish an ambulance," Staudt had offered.

Pascal had sworn at him and had lifted the shrouded corpse of his sister from the table. Staggering, the boy had put it across his shoulder while his mother moaned and pleaded with him not to defile his sister's memory but to let the Major help them.

"They have helped Sylvie enough already," Pascal Fromont had snapped.

It had been too much for Staudt, too comically obscene. He had barred the boy's unsteady exit from the basement.

"Be it as you wish. But I will not permit you to lug her like—to take her thus. What do you need? A motor? Can you drive?"

"No."

"I will give you—"

"Get me a cart, that's all," Pascal had said.

Staudt had called for two troopers to carry the wrapped body into the rear yard of the town hall, out of sight of the crowd. He had no desire to offer the townsfolk a martyr. He had provided the cart, had had two troopers lift the girl's body on to it, had stood silently while the slender French boy struggled with the shafts and, with his mother walking a yard ahead, had trundled the cart out of the courtyard and into the back streets, with Staudt's letter of clearance clenched in his teeth like a bit.

The Obergruppenführer would not have allowed it. The devil take Ribbeck, Staudt thought, as the Fromonts passed out of his sight into the lane; I have done what is right.

Sturmbannführer Staudt never did discover that what he had done, by way of noble gesture, was to create the circumstances that Jeff Deacon would ascribe to luck.

It was Pascal Fromont that Mayor Guizot encountered as he sneaked along St. Félice's tree-lined boulevards. Pascal Fromont who told him where Paget was to be found and, handing the cart shafts to his dumbstruck mother, raced away towards the corn mill to inform Lisa that the British had not let them down.

Panting and pained by a stitch in his side, Mayor Guizot jogged as fast as his trembling legs would carry him, hoping to reach the field track on the Melampyre road before the two British soldiers grew tired of waiting.

SS troopers were much in evidence along the Boulevard de Champagne and in the long Avenue de Paris. Fortunately, Guizot was headed away from the advancing patrols and, after ten minutes, lost sight of them. By then he was in the suburbs, such as they were, and could see fields and lush green trees peeking through the bungalows.

When the black Mercedes hurtled out of the corner of the Melampyre road, however, Guizot was caught completely by surprise. He had no opportunity to take cover—which, as it happened, was a stroke of excellent good fortune.

"There's the Frog," shouted P.B. McNair.

Buz braked. The massive sedan swerved to a halt. Glancing behind him, Buz saw the elderly Frenchman scuttle for cover in a privet hedge. He flung open the door. Leaned out and yelled, "*Guizot. Guizot. It's us.*"

Guizot had got himself entangled in the hedge and, in the throes of exhaustion, could not extricate himself. Buz backed the Mercedes up to him, climbed from the car and went over to the mayor.

"Found ourselves wheels," Buz said. "And a kraut general to give us a passport. What's the news, monsieur?"

Breathlessly, Mayor Guizot told the sergeant how he had encountered Pascal Fromont and that Paget was hidden in an abandoned corn mill not far off.

"What about our lieutenant?"

"I know nothing of him."

"Right," said Buz. "We'll go get Paget and worry about our guy later. How far is the ride?"

"Minutes," said Guizot, as Buz helped him across the pavement and into the car.

The French mayor and the German general regarded each other with calm detestation.

"Know him?" Buz asked.

"No. He is not the officer who issued the order for our detention," said Guizot. "That was a Major Staudt."

"Hoy, Adolf, what's *your* fuckin' name?" said P.B. McNair, taking a direct approach.

"It will be an end of your town," said Ribbeck to Guizot. "*St. Félice is finished.*"

"I'm talkin' to you, Adolf," said P.B. McNair.

"I am SS Obergruppenführer Josef Ribbeck," said the general, addressing himself to Guizot and ignoring the corporal by his side. "I have friends of influence. If I am not set free at once the consequences will be fatal. Do you understand my meaning?"

"Enough of it," said Guizot.

"My tanks will open fire. Nobody will escape. Tell these British fools to release me."

"Where's the mill, monsieur?" said Buz.

"Make a turn to your left and then another to your right," Guizot told the sergeant.

Buz drove the Mercedes at a sedate pace.

"What do you hope to gain?" said Ribbeck. "There can be no escape for any of you."

"What's he bletherin' about?" said P.B. McNair.

"He is urging me to help set him free and promising dreadful consequences if I do not," said Guizot.

"What do you think of his offer?" asked Buz.

"I do not trade with swine," said the mayor and then, with a smile, repeated his statement in German and turned abruptly to face the windscreen. "Turn left again, sergeant. Be careful, there are Nazi patrols in the area."

"Is that the place? That big old building?" asked Buz.

"Yes, that is the corn mill. It has not been used for eight or nine years, not since the modern plant opened in—"

"Buz, there's Deacon," said P.B.

"Yeah, I see him. All in one piece too."

The lieutenant, Webley in hand, was half-hidden by a gatepost. He ducked out of sight as soon as he spotted the Mercedes. Buz chuckled, accelerated and bucked the sedan into the courtyard at the front of the mill building. He had caught the kid with his pants down. They were bringing Paget out of the mill. Three of them, a guy with a moustache, a boy and a gorgeous-looking girl.

"That is Lisa Vandeleur," said Guizot.

Tamping the car horn in salute, Buz rolled the Mercedes round the courtyard and brought it smoothly to a halt by the side door through which, in musty gloom, the partisans had frantically manhandled the stretcher.

Buz flung open the car's nearside door.

"Any more for the Skylark," he shouted.

Smiling, Jeff Deacon stepped from cover.

"Where the devil have you been, sergeant?"

"Here and there," said Buz. "Got your boy?"

"He's in a pretty bad way," said Deacon, peering into the car. "Good Lord, an Obergruppenführer. That's a find."

"With him on board we'll run out free and easy," said Buz.

"You," said Ribbeck, snapping his head towards Deacon and speaking German. "You are the officer?"

"I am," Deacon answered.

"There is no hope for any of you. German panzer divisions

stretch from here to the Channel coast. All ports are in German hands and the Allied forces have been destroyed."

Deacon gave a little bow and clicked his heels. "I thank you for the information, Herr General. My German is adequate to most occasions. I regret, however, that I must respond by using an Americanism. I am sure that you will understand." Deacon's smile waxed. "*Bullshit*, Herr General. *Bullshit!*"

5 Run to the sea

ON A PEACEFUL SUMMER'S DAY, Deacon could have driven to the coast in under an hour, but Ribbeck had told no lie; the Allied armies, in disarray, had been driven back to the coastal ports by the panzer divisions. The thirty-one miles that separated St. Félice from the sea seemed like a thousand.

Strapped with webbing to the palliasse, Paget was laid at full length on the rear seat of the Mercedes. Lisa and P.B. McNair, on jump seats, were instructed to hold him still. On the front bench seat were Campbell, at the wheel, Deacon and the Obergruppen-führer. Ribbeck's wrists were roped to the doorhandle to prevent him making a desperate bid to thrust himself against Buz and run the Mercedes off the road. Deacon was armed with the Webley and one of the Lugers. A second Luger was tucked handily into Buz Campbell's blouse, the rest of the weapons lay on the floor of the rear compartment.

Georges administered the last of his stock of morphine a minute before departure and adjusted the webbing around Paget's broken thigh. The scientist was conscious and rational enough to thank the horse-doctor for all that he had done, promising, without conviction, that they would meet again when the war was over.

Georges also spoke with Lisa and promised her that he would look after her father and ensure that the partisans got safely out of the district now that their cover had been blown.

"Paris," said Georges. "We will all make it to Paris. After that, who knows!"

"Papa—give him my love. Tell him I will see him in Paris, soon."

"But of course." Georges hugged the girl then pushed her into the car and slammed the door. "Take care, my dear."

"You too," said Lisa tearfully.

Buz waited no longer. He made a U-turn and headed the sedan out of the yard of the corn mill, leaving the two Frenchmen and the boy, Pascal, behind.

Slouched against the locked door, Ribbeck said, "They will not get away. None of them will evade justice."

"Don't be so sure," said Deacon.

"The girl?" Ribbeck spoke in rapid German. "She is Vandeleur's daughter?"

"What of it?" said Deacon.

Ribbeck smiled slyly. "Vandeleur was shot dead not half an hour ago in the Rue Picarde."

"What did he say?" asked Lisa from the rear seat.

"Why don't you answer her?" said Ribbeck.

"There's no need for her to know," said Deacon.

"What did he say about me?" Lisa persisted.

"Are you that much of a coward, lieutenant?" said Ribbeck.

"He was asking if you were Lisa Vandeleur, that's all." Deacon kept his eyes on Ribbeck, saying "If you open your mouth once more, Herr General, I will take great delight in removing several of your teeth with my pistol butt."

"The other, the corporal—perhaps. But not you. You are a gentleman."

Deacon smashed the butt of the Webley against Ribbeck's upper lip. The general grovelled against the door, crying out in pain and astonishment. Blood oozed from broken flesh.

"Next time," said Deacon softly, "it's teeth."

Ribbeck licked the flow of blood and spat into the footwell, viciously, his eyes hard and malevolent.

"What's with you?" Buz had been distracted by the sudden outburst.

"He insulted me," said Deacon. "I don't like to be slandered by a German, even if he is a general."

Ribbeck spat again.

Buz said, "Hold on to your hats, folks. There's a patrol up front."

Jerking his head, Buz shook off his service cap. Deacon stooped low, holding the Webley against Ribbeck's side. "Take it slow, Buz," he said.

"Right."

There were eight foot soldiers in SS uniform and a back-up vehicle with a machine gun in it. The unit pulled in against the pavement as the Mercedes approached and the NCO in charge saluted stiffly. Pennants flying, the sedan roared past.

Leaning across Paget, P.B. peered out of the back window.

"Lookin' at us a bit funny," P.B. announced.

"Are they following us?" asked Deacon.

"No. They're gone back towards the houses."

"One up," Buz steered the car round the long, tree-lined curve of the avenue and swung left into the high road to Quern. "But beating the road-block won't be so easy."

"Do we bluff it?" said Deacon.

"Do we, fuck!" said Buz Campbell. "Not with this slippery geezer on board."

"How will we get past the block?" Lisa asked.

"Brute force," said Buz.

Three minutes later, after passing two more units, the road-block came into view.

"Do I have your permission to accelerate, sir?" Buz winked at Deacon.

"Put your foot to the floor, sergeant."

"Thank you, sir." Leaning forward, Buz squeezed his boot-sole gently upon the pedal and touched the big proud snout of the Mercedes into the exact center of the road. "Hold tight in the back there."

The sight of expensive staff cars was familiar not only to officers but to most of the rank and file of the SS Totenkopf, a regiment which flaunted its class at every opportunity. They were trained to treat the vehicles with a respect that amounted to reverence and no action was taken to prevent the sedan's progress. On the contrary, the roadway was cleared as soon as the sedan appeared and the barricade would have been manned for immediate lifting if the staff car had shown any signs of slowing down. Blame could hardly be attached to the bewildered NCOs who stood idly by as the Mercedes ploughed into and through the barrier that defended the road to Quern.

There was almost no impact, no shock transmitted through the car's plating as the snubbed bonnet cleft the wooden post and neatly snapped it. A section rattled harmlessly on the windscreen, making Deacon blink, then the road-block, hut, guards and all were behind them and Buz was giving the Mercedes the gun, boosting the supercharged engine up gear by gear until the gray highway streamed towards them like a ribbon and the speedometer needle quivered on ninety.

Deacon had no opportunity to gauge the effect on the sentries. It occurred to him that the Mercedes would be at the Quern canal in about ten minutes, long before decisions could be taken, pursuit ordered. If their luck held, and the highway remained clear, they might even overtake one of the retreating BEF units. They might even weasel through the German lines into Calais or Dunkirk, sail past the panzers sheltered by the Obergruppenführer's pennants and gaudy Nazi eagle.

"How's Paget?" Deacon called out.

Lisa answered, "Very good, so far."

"I do believe we're going to make it," Deacon said.

But one mile east of the Quern canal they ran into the scouting tanks and Deacon realized that his optimism had been rather premature.

SS Sturmbannführer Staudt quit the office and stalked angrily out of the town hall into the square. A mobile radio van was drawn up below the steps, its rear door open. Staudt climbed in and closed the door behind him. Hauptsturmführer Wester was already there. Face expressionless, he held the receiver of a field telephone in one hand. Backed into the cramped corner of the van were two soldiers, rumpled and sweaty.

"Is this true, Wester?" Staudt demanded.

"Yes, Obergruppenführer Ribbeck has been taken prisoner by a British raiding party."

"Who is on the line?"

"Sergeant Brôckner, sir, from the road-block on the Quern road."

Staudt snatched the telephone. "I am Sturmbannführer Staudt. What is this you have to report?"

The major listened, asked, "How long is it since the general's staff car broke through the road block?"

"How long, sir?" whispered Wester.

Staudt held up five fingers.

"God in Heaven!" said Wester. "They will be halfway to the coast by now."

"Was the general in the car?" asked Staudt of the guard sergeant. "Did you see him with your own eyes?"

"Did he?" asked Wester.

Staudt nodded.

"How long ago did our scout tanks pass through?"

Staudt nodded once more then instructed the guard sergeant to repair and re-man the barrier. He gave the worried NCO no comfort and hung up immediately. He slammed his fist into the van's steel wall then spun towards the cowering soldiers in the corner.

"You," Staudt pointed at the elder man. "Tell me quickly what happened at the farm and what you saw on the road."

The nervous private stiffened and tried to rise, then, urged into coherence by the major, rattled off an account of the surprise attack at Melampyre.

"How long ago did this happen?"

"Half an hour, sir. Forty minutes. No longer."

"Why did you not make for a radio?"

"I—we could not find one, sir."

"Did you hide?"

"No, no, Herr Sturmbannführer."

"Liar!" said Staudt. "Get out of here, both of you. Wester, see that they make detailed reports, without excuses or exaggerations."

"Yes, Herr Sturmbannführer."

"And find Mauseberg at once."

"Sir." Wester herded the privates out of the van and led them into the building.

Staudt remained in the van with the radio operator who, with his back to the proceedings, had already opened a channel of communication to Command Headquarters in Lille.

But Staudt had other ideas.

"Get me Luftwaffe Attack Group Three, corporal."

"Luftwaffe Attack Group Three."

A couple of minutes later, a cigarette smoking in his fingers, Staudt was in conversation with a Luftwaffe squadron commander with whom, to his disgust, he became involved in an argument.

"I have my own authority," Staudt shouted. "I tell you the black Mercedes staff car with the general's emblems on it must be stopped. Yes, bomb the road around it. Yes, it is a risk, I realize. Yes, I will take responsibility if the car is damaged. No, I do not have higher authority. SS Obergruppenführer Ribbeck is not here." Tactfully Staudt did not inform the Luftwaffe senior officer that Ribbeck was a passenger in the black Mercedes. "The car has been stolen and is full of English officers. Escapers, yes."

At length the squadron commander agreed to send two planes into the area with instructions to search for and halt the staff car.

Before Hauptsturmführer Mauseberg arrived, Staudt had contacted the field headquarters of three panzer divisions in the sector through which the Mercedes would travel if it left the Quern road east of the canal. He gave explicit orders as to what was to be done if the general's Mercedes was encountered and, as a sop to the purpose of the mission, suggested that all the occupants of the sedan be taken alive—if possible.

He thanked the radio operator, opened the van door and stepped down into afternoon sunlight.

The square looked indecently peaceful. The hour appointed for Ribbeck's executions had come and gone and tension, so Staudt thought, had eased from the crowd. The civilians were seated around the railings and on the grass of the little park. Only a small number, less than a hundred, remained near the town hall steps. His presence did not appear to disturb them, nor did the proximity of the tanks. He could not comprehend such passivity.

Mauseberg arrived on the double. He had been lunching when Wester had found him. Wester had brought the company commander up to date and Mauseberg, a panzer, had thoughtfully brought along his adjutant, dressed in the black garb of a fighting man.

"Do you wish me to destroy the town now, Herr Sturm-bannführer?"

"As an act of reprisal?" said Staudt, grimly. "Is that what you would do, Mauseberg?"

"It is what the Obergruppenführer would do."

"I am aware of that," answered Staudt.

He looked around the square. At last the activity had impinged itself and townsfolk were gathering, nervously, around the park railings. The guards were tense too, their weapons at the ready.

"How long would it take to kill them?" asked Staudt.

"All of them?"

"A majority?"

"Ten minutes."

"And how long would it take to have the panzers on the move?"

"Ten minutes."

"Draw up the panzers, Mauseberg. We are moving out of St. Félice."

"But what about them?" Mauseberg waved his hand in the direction of the crowd.

"Send them home."

"But, Staudt—?"

"We will head for Quern," said Staudt. "If the canal is not passable there, we will travel north to the bridge at Muellen and rejoin the main thrust of Totenkopf tanks at Bovet, in which direction they are presently travelling. The BEF are contained in a pocket with their backs to the sea at Dunkirk. I want to be there, with the regiment, at the kill."

Mauseberg smiled in delight.

He saluted.

"Will you lead us, Herr Sturmbannführer?"

"In the absence of the Obergruppenführer, yes, I will lead."

"I will have a staff car brought round."

"Mauseberg," said Staudt, "I believe I will travel in a command vehicle."

"Most wise, Staudt," said the Hauptsturmführer.

"Make ready," Staudt ordered, and with a sigh of relief looked round for the megaphone.

* * *

When Buz saw the German tanks a quarter of a mile ahead he brought down the Mercedes' speed as discreetly as possible. The tanks were PzKpfw IIs, agile beasts but lacking basic speed and with poor vision from the turrets. Not all were equipped with radios but he figured that those on scout work would have some means of contacting base. The tanks were not supported by infantry. Impatiently Buz sounded the car horn. Maybe a general's insignia would be enough to induce the tanks to pull over.

Buz glanced at Ribbeck. The kraut had gotten himself forward in the seat. Stretched to the limit of his tethers, he watched the tanks expectantly. Buz tamped the horn once more and flicked the headlights. The trail tank slowed and halted, smack in the center of the road. The hatch opened. The commander put his head out, then, recognizing the staff car, hoisted himself up and saluted.

"What do we do now, lieutenant?" Buz whispered.

"Try bluff."

Deacon leaned across Ribbeck, screwed down the window and called out a German instruction ordering the tanks to move over and make way for SS Obergruppenführer Ribbeck who was in a tearing hurry to reach Quern.

The panzer commander jumped down from the turret. He marched smartly towards the Mercedes.

"Hit," Buz asked, "or run?"

"God knows!" said Deacon.

"Make up your mind quick," said Buz.

Ribbeck thrust his face towards the open window and shouted five or six words before P.B. snapped a webbing strap around his gullet and jerked his head back.

"*Run*," Deacon cried.

Buz missed the gear shift. Caught in indecision, the panzer hesitated then came on again. From the lead tank, just visible, another panzer emerged. Buz found gear. The Mercedes shot backwards. The tank commander yelled and ran after them, waving, then, as the Mercedes continued its erratic course down the country road, turned and hared towards his tank.

Buz navigated by the mirror.

Deacon said, "Don't kill him, P.B. Let him breathe."

P.B. released the strap lightly and allowed the Obergruppen-führer to suck in a lungful of air.

Lisa cried out, "The ditch."

The Mercedes bounced and wavered. Buz adjusted its line, zigzagging the vehicle around a curve out of sight of the tanks.

"What the hell did Ribbeck say?" Buz asked.

"'English soldiers. I am a captive,'" said Deacon.

"Leastways we know they hadn't had a radio message to look out for us," said Buz.

"But they will now, will they not?" said Lisa. "The panzers will report."

"How do we get off this goddamned road?" said Buz. "Jesus, at this rate we'll be back in St. Félice in ten minutes."

"There's a farm track a half-mile back, Buz. It'll take us off the highway on to the ridge."

"What good'll that do? You want to lay up?"

"I'd prefer to keep going," said Deacon. "But I suspect the bridge at Quern is still down. It's only eight hours since we blew it, remember."

"Who could forget!" Buz growled.

"Twelve miles north," said Deacon, "there's another bridge on the Rue Bovet. We may have to try for that one. There, Buz, that's the farm road."

Buz drove up the incline. It was hardly more than a track marked out with hedges. Deacon fished out his map and pored over it. Ribbeck, head still craned back by the pressure of the webbing strap, rasped beside him. In the back, Paget groaned. Lisa talked to him in English.

It was, Buz thought, all pretty crazy. He felt like the driver of an international nut-house collecting van.

"Know where we are?" he asked.

"A couple of miles," said Deacon, "should bring us to the farmhouse—where the road ends."

"*What?*"

"We're on the side of a hill," said Deacon. "Le Mont des Poulets. Roughtly translated that means Chickens' Hill."

"Ain't that appropriate?" Buz said. "What do you hope to find up here? Eggs?"

"Perhaps Lisa can persuade the farmer to lend us a less obvious mode of transport," said Deacon.

"It is a feeble hope, Jeff," said the girl.

"It's better than being caught on the high road," said Deacon.

But there was no farm, no farmer—only chickens, and most of the chickens were dead. The farmhouse had been a target for heavy shelling. Chicken-runs smashed, the dead birds were strewn over the grass like clots of foam. By a deep crater lay two cows, both dead. A water spigot had snapped, turning the road into a river of reddish mud. Precious little remained of the farmhouse, a hanging wall, a bed upturned on mounds of debris. Smoke spewed from burning outbuildings.

Nobody in the Mercedes spoke as Buz drove past.

Ahead there was nothing but sky, sky and smoke and furze bushes in bright yellow flower. Surviving chickens scratched the peaceful plot and a donkey, an aged little creature, brayed and tottered off at the car's approach.

"End of the line." Buz stopped the sedan at a gate that fed into the pasture.

"Let me out, Buz," said Deacon.

"I'll come with you," said Buz. "Wee man, keep the kraut's collar on."

Sergeant and lieutenant walked from the Mercedes into the bushes where they relieved themselves. Then Deacon went on, following a footpath through the furze on to the north-facing slope. He was back within a minute.

"Come and see this, sergeant."

Before Buz could go after Deacon, however, they were joined by the girl.

"I am able to help with the geography, Jeff," Lisa said. "May I come with you?"

"Of course," Deacon said.

He led the couple to a gap in the bushes.

Rough pasture swept down to the plain. The Quern canal seemed to be directly beneath them. Straight and narrow as the road to Paradise, it shimmered metallically in muted afternoon sunlight. In the middle distance pontoon bridges crossed the waterway where the Germans appeared to be holding a reserve line. Mobile cook-houses sent up the savoury smell of hot food. Queues of troops waited to be served. Tanks, light and heavy weights, were leaguered in an attack formation, mechanics and supply units busy as ants.

"Over there," said Deacon.

"What the hell is it?"

Deacon handed Buz the field-glasses.

"The sea."

The far distant line of glassy blue was just visible, like a mirage.

"What about Quern?" asked Lisa. "Has it been occupied again?"

The three moved south along the breast of the hill until they were able to look down upon the town. The bridge had not been replaced though German engineers were already unloading materials from heavy trucks. Across the canal, in Quern, panzers rested, lining the quays, eating and drinking, sleeping with their heads on the stones. The citizens of Quern had returned. Through the glasses Buz saw a stall selling fruit and another dispensing beer.

"That didn't take long, did it?" said Deacon.

"It's occupied by army units, though," Buz said. "Not SS. Not the Totenkopf."

"Bovet is over there," said Lisa, pointing.

In the sunshine, on the hill, she looked very young. Her dark hair was glossy and her breasts showed taut against the shirting.

"How far is Bovet, Lisa?"

"Fifteen miles, once we have crossed the canal."

"Congested as hell all the way, no doubt."

"Yeah," said Buz, "but there will be movement of sorts. Traffic police will keep the panzer supplies flowing. There won't be much fighting in this sector now. If you ask me, lieutenant, the BEF has its back to the English Channel."

"The evacuation must be in full swing," said Deacon, "so we daren't dally too long."

Lisa said, "It will be impossible to travel in the German staff car, especially as you are wearing British uniform."

"I'm afraid we'll have to wait until darkness falls," said Deacon, "before we can risk crossing the canal."

"It ain't on," said Buz Campbell. "We've been spotted in this area. There's bound to be a search, maybe from the air."

"We could hide the Mercedes, I suppose," Deacon suggested.

"What we need is an ambulance," Buz said.

"How on earth do we get one of those?"

"Steal one," said Buz.

"In broad daylight?"

"Unless I'm mistaken," Buz said, "there's a field hospital only a mile down the road."

Deacon raised the binoculars and scanned the road that followed the line of the canal on the east bank.

"By God, Buz, you're right."

"P.B. and me, we'll go get the ambulance. You bring the Mercedes down the side of the hill. Think you can manage it?"

Deacon studied the pasture; it was steep but he could see no major impediments and the sedan was build for rough treatment. He said, "Why not?"

"Right," said Buz. "That farm, to our right, on the little track—it looks deserted. We'll meet up there in half an hour."

Deacon glanced at Lisa.

The girl shrugged.

"I wish I could think of an alternative," Deacon said.

"But you can't, can you?"

"No."

"Then my plan is on?"

"Yes."

"One ambulance," Buz said, "coming right up."

Dielman and Heincke were a couple of general dogsbodies in the Deutsche Rote Kreuz. The German Red Cross organization had been brought under control of the National Socialists and tricked out with new uniforms and a wonderful range of rank badges. Even the lowliest medical attendant, the humblest driver, fair bristled with pips and flashes and bars of silver lace which, with dove-grey uniforms and jackboots, made a man proud to be a Nazi even when he was emptying bedpans, wiping up vomit or toting dismembered corpses back from battlefields for identification and burial.

DRK man Dielman and his companion, Heincke, were a couple of blockheads who had chummed up as far back as 1934 when they had met as janitors in the Frankfurt General Hospital. They thought of themselves, even while whoring and drinking, as Angels of Mercy, and worshipped all doctors as gods. To give them their due, they were efficient and caring when it came down to handling the victims of war, but their humanitarianism stopped short of handing over their field ambulance to a couple of haggard Britons.

Dielman and Heincke had worked like beavers all morning, ferrying dead and dying panzers back from Dunkirk. Six "hopeless cases" were carried each trip, strapped into hammocks rigged in the back of the Granit 25, an uncomfortable vehicle with a folding cab top and canvas curtain. Dielman and Heincke hoped to trade it in for an Adler or an open Blitz before much longer. Dielman and Heincke had made two trips to the "clearing house" at Bovet that morning. On the first trip of the day they had had the company of four DRK nurses and there had been much hilarity in spite of the early hour. On the trip back to the line camp on the Quern canal they had six dying men on board and two DRK nurses, real "angels of mercy," as Heincke remarked, who could pluck his harp any night if they wanted the practice.

It was almost 2 p.m. before Dielman and Heincke were sent to the mess by General Officer Rustow. Ordered to be on the road again by 2.30, they would pick up their Granit at the park in the back of the fuel depot and make directly for Bovet for a third and last trip before stand-down.

Heincke had made a date with one of the DRK nurses and pressed his chum to bolt dinner and get on the road early so that there might be no delay in returning. Heincke planned to show the nurse the sights of Quern and ply her with much strong red wine before dragging her into the bushes along the canal bank. The nurse had a fine dark moustache which Heincke found irresistible and over which he enthused at geat length during their hasty meal.

Heincke was still rabbiting on about his hirsute venus—Dielman had switched off ages ago—when the pair reached the vehicle park where, close to the trees, the Granit waited, windscreen washed, tires infalted, its tank brimful with gas.

It was Dielman's turn to drive.

Dielman clambered through the canvas flap and seated himself behind the wheel. A short thick cigar was stuck in his mouth and he puffed noisily as he waited for Heincke to make his desultory check of the ambulance and join him in the cab. Dielman didn't even glance up when the side flap lifted. He was stooped forward, fitting the key into the awkwardly placed ignition on the steering column when the gun butt descended on his medulla oblongata. The cigar shot out of Dielman's mouth like a tiny torpedo and for the next hour or so the DRK man knew no more.

Heincke was a shade less fortunate.

Regulations dictated that the contents of the ambulance be checked after each trip, blankets, belts and medical supplies replaced if necessary. Before the day's first run, Dielman or Heincke would perform this chore thoroughly but thereafter they were content to hoist the curtain, run their eye over the bedding, and let the curtain fall again.

Heincke hoisted up the curtain.

Hands gripped his throat, yanked him from the grass and slammed his face down upon the tailgate plate. He squealed and kicked as the hands changed position, clasped his ears, lifted his head like a jug and broke it on the Granit's side wall. Heincke's eyes darted like guppies in a bowl. But Heincke had a skull of iron. He did not pass out.

"Christ, what's wrong wi' you?"

The language was unfamiliar to DRK man Heincke and seemed more brutal, more guttural and more primitive than any German dialect, even Swabian.

"Die, y'bastard."

Heincke would have been delighted to pass swiftly and competently into oblivion. But he could not. His skull rattled again on the metal upright. He was pulled into the Granit's dim interior. The stench of antiseptics and a general odor of death assailed him vividly. He tried to protect his poor head from further punishment and whimpered for Dielman to save him. Immediately his arms were pinned to the floor and weight bore down on the small of his back.

Confused, terrified and dazed though he was, Heincke recognized the cold kiss of a Luger against his neck.

"One word, Hermann, just one fuckin' word—"

Heincke lay very still.

Beneath his belly he felt the shudder of the Granit's engine, heard the odd growl it emitted on starting, the squeak of grit in the suspension leaves and the familiar *yawp* that the transmission gave out when first connected.

Heincke could not help himself.

Through swollen lips the words slithered out.

"God in Heaven!" Heincke gasped in amazement. "They are stealing our ambulance."

At which point something heavy belted the back of his neck and, at last, DRK man Heincke blacked out.

Minutes, hours or days? The pair had no way of gauging time for their watches had been removed along with everything else. The buzzing of a nasty black fly wakened Dielman who, groaning, wakened Heincke. The pair groaned in unison for a moment, each lashed by head pains and totally disorientated. Finally the black fly gave Dielman focus. He concentrated on its flight against pink splinters of sky.

The fly droned down and rested in Dielman's navel.

Dielman wriggled. In reflex he tried to move his hand to swat away the offensive insect. His hand would not move. His legs would not move. He was paralyzed. He cried out in fear. The fly goose-stepped across his white belly towards his groin.

"They have taken everything," said Heincke. "Look, we are naked."

Dielman surveyed the landscape of his body in amazement.

"Who has done this?" he asked.

"It was not the nurses," said Heincke.

"My head, my head! God, my head!"

Dielman squirmed.

His hands and arms were bound tightly with bandages, knees, ankles, feet bound too. He squinted at the naked Heincke who was similarly trussed up.

"Where—where are we?"

"Listen. Shelling. So we are not in England."

"It is still France. What shall we do?"

"Shout."

"HEEEEEEELLLLP!" bawled Dielman. "Oh, my head!"

"They have taken everything. But why? And when will we be found?"

"Not tonight, perhaps. See, it's almost sundown."

"We'll shout together. Ready?"

"HEEELLLP. SAVE US. HEEELLP."

Dusk deepened and night fell.

The intrepid DRK men shouted singly and in tandem until their skulls turned to brass and their throats to parchment. As they had been dumped a good two miles from the line camp on the wrong flank of the Mont des Poulets, nobody heard them. Fitfully they slept through the night but had to wait until mid-morning to be discovered by two giggling young French girls who at least had the wit to untie them before scampering away.

It was noon before Dielman and Heincke limped into camp, naked and exhausted, to report the theft of their ambulance.

By that time the Granit and its heartless abductors were, of course, long gone.

From his vantage point on the breast of the Mont des Poulets, Deacon watched Operation Ambulance through the binoculars. He left Lisa to keep an eye on Paget who, now that the car had come to rest, was sleeping peacefully enough. Though Ribbeck was securely tied to the doorhandle, not having the German in sight made Deacon nervous. He was afraid that the general might inform Lisa that her father was dead. Later, when they were safely back in England, Deacon intended to break the news to her as gently as possible.

Swiftly and stealthily down the side of the hill Campbell and McNair travelled across the diagonal field to a coppice at the rear of the German encampment. No guards were posted on the camp's perimeters. Perhaps the victorious panzers felt they had no need to squander manpower in daylight hours. Buz and P.B. vanished like shadows into the clump of trees. Deacon saw no more of them. For thirty-five minutes he waited, watching alertly. One of the ambulances started. He followed its progress anxiously as it prowled across a corner of the park, emerged on to the canal road, turned south and immediately picked up speed. When it turned left along the farm track at the base of the Mont des Poulets, Deacon scrambled for cover and ran back to the Mercedes.

Lisa was seated on the grass, a Luger in her hand, twenty yards from the Mercedes. Ribbeck, Deacon was pleased to note, had fallen asleep, head slumped against the window.

"They've got it. They've pilfered a damned ambulance for us," Deacon said. "All we have to do now is manoeuvre this monster downhill and we can ride in comfort through the German lines. In theory, at least."

"It will be a rough ride, no?" said Lisa.

"Very," said Deacon. "Can you hold Paget in place, not allow him to get too knocked about?"

"Of course."

"And," said Deacon, "keep an eye on Herr Ribbeck. I don't trust that gentleman. With only two of us in the car he might just decide to do something stupid."

"I will watch him carefully, Jeff."

With Lisa and Paget in the rear and Ribbeck beside him on the front bench, Deacon started up the Mercedes.

The sedan behaved magnificently. It was engineered for heavy duty and equipped with broad tires that gripped the grass slope admirably. The small farm on the side road was no more than six hundred yards away. The incline measured about 1 in 5. As a bonus, a tree plantation screened the car's descent from sight of the encampment—but not from the sky. The Mercedes was halfway down the hill when the Stukas zoomed overhead, two of them, flying close and low.

Wide awake now, Ribbeck showed his teeth and, squirming against his bonds, squinted up through the windscreen at the aircraft.

Deacon held the car in line. He had chosen a route close to the trees. It rocked and bounced over the rough terrain. In the rear, Paget cried out as the motion of the car socked into his body. Lisa braced herself on her knees and held the injured scientist in her arms, protecting him as best she could.

Ribbeck grinned evilly at Deacon.

"Do you see? The Luftwaffe are searching for us. You cannot escape."

"Shut up," Deacon snapped.

A towering blackthorn hedge sealed the pasture above the track. The lieutenant was none too keen to charge down it. On the far side the bank above the track was steep. He was increasingly aware of Paget's distress. He pulled from the shadow of the trees and nosed the sedan across the corner of the hill pasture towards the farm. He could not see the roof now but had carefully marked its location with reference to the geometry of the hedges. He was a quarter of a mile too far west. Rutted ground flung the Mercedes about mercilessly. Deacon slowed. After the pull of the descent he felt as if it had practically come to a standstill.

The Mercedes was running parallel to the hedgerow when the Stukas returned.

"Damn!" said Deacon. "Damn, damn, damn!"

"You will be stopped," Ribbeck crowed. "You will all be shot. I will personally see to it. All shot."

"Bloody shut up!" Deacon shouted.

At that precise moment the first bombs fell.

Mud sprayed the windscreen, wedges of earth thudded on the roof, loose pebbles rattled across the bonnet. Startled, Ribbeck dragged against the ropes and cowered into the footwell. The Obergruppenführer's reaction was so unexpected that Deacon's rage evaporated. Smoke from the bomb blasts wafted over them. Deacon stopped the Mercedes short of the craters.

"My God! My God!" Ribbeck muttered. "They will come again. They will destroy us. They cannot know that I am here."

Deacon turned. "Lisa, we must get Paget out of here. I'll give you a hand. We'll put him on the stretcher by the side of the hedge, out of sight. When the Stukas go past again, cut for the little farm. Leave Paget. You can't carry him. Campbell and the Scot should be at the farm with the ambulance. They'll fetch Paget and take him on board."

"Jeff, what about—?"

"Wait at the farm until I've gone, then follow me in the ambulance. Turn left at the end of the track, away from the German camp. Do you understand me?"

"Jeff. No, you cannot."

"Don't damned well argue, girl."

Lisa opened the rear door.

Deacon ran round, helped her draw out the stretcher and lay it in the grasses at the foot of the thorn hedge. He got to his feet, leapt high to see over the hedge. What sort of effect would the bomb run have on the German panzers? Would they automatically send out a mopping-up detail?

"Paget, hang on," he said; then to Lisa, "Do you have a gun?"

"Yes, a Luger. But, Jeff—"

"Duck! Here they come again." Deacon dived back into the car.

Ribbeck was in a state of funk; there was no other word for it. The big cheese in the SS was wetting himself with fear. Deacon felt a momentary pang of pity for the old devil. Being tied to the inside of a moving vehicle in the middle of a field while a couple of Stukas lined up on you was no joke. Deacon flung the Mercedes into reverse gear, shot it away from the hedge and ploughed an uphill course back towards the trees.

The Stukas had wheeled in a flattened circle to make the bombing run along the same path as before. He could see them plainly from the side window, darting along the surface of the grass like gigantic dragonflies. The noise hit him. Deacon's gut clenched as the shadows of the planes flew over him and the whistling bombs fell. He tramped on the accelerator and swung the sedan away from the target zone, away from the spot where Paget and Lisa lay.

The bombs burst behind the car. Blasts shoved the two-ton sedan forward on a wave of dirt and turf. Deacon flung himself against the steering wheel, roared the engine and drove straight uphill. He spared a moment's attention for the mirror. Lisa was running fast along the hedge line, debris falling like rain in her wake.

"Let me out. My God, you pig, you English pig! Do you intend me to die too?" Ribbeck thrashed against the ropes and beat his head against the window like a petulant child. "I order you to release me."

The Mercedes was two hundred yards uphill, high on the hillside, when Deacon made the turn. Ropes biting into his wrists, Ribbeck scrabbled to fit his bulk into the footwell. Facing Deacon, his eagle-like features eroded by terror, he screamed, *"No, you cannot."*

Deacon felt extraordinarily calm. He supposed it had something to do with the amount of adrenalin swilling about in his system. What lay beyond the hedge was anybody's guess. It could be a lime pit or a duck pond or a twenty-foot drop, a minefield or an abandoned tank. He could see nothing. He transferred his foot from brake to accelerator and pressed down hard.

The Stukas levelled off on an eliptical curve and came downwind from the west, low over the trees.

Fifty yards behind the Mercedes, bombs gouged an erratic pattern of craters. Earth deluged the car once more.

Deacon aimed the bonnet at the thorn hedge. The car bucked wildly. The wheel danced between Deacon's fingertips. The hedge loomed closer. The hedge rushed upon him.

The sedan lifted, the farm track below, hedge opposite.

Deacon snapped the steering on to full lock.

The car landed with a bone-jarring shock. The impetus flung Deacon forward. He cracked his brow upon the dash and, for an instant, lost control. The sedan charged on, demolished a great section of the hedge, careered broadside, then spun off the banking. Deacon had recovered enough to clench the wheel again. He brought the car on to the track and headed it away from the little farm towards the canal road.

Blood seeped into his eye from a contused wound at the hairline. He dabbed with his sleeve and grunted. Glancing right, he saw that Ribbeck, though battered, was not seriously hurt. The general hauled himself on to the seat again.

The car reached the road end. Deacon made a left turn on two wheels. He imagined that he had escaped the dive-bombers and all he would have to contend with now was the panzers. But Deacon did not know of the SS Sturmbannführer's order to kill. He had covered less than a half-mile towards Quern, on the canal road, when the Stukas winged in once more.

Deacon saw them very clearly; spatted undercarriages, cranked wings. They swooped like hunting hawks along the treetops. They had perfect range and clearance—and the pilots were good. Hitting the diving brakes to balance the run, low and steady they threaded the gap on streamers of sound and seeded the asphalt with machine-gun fire. A string of bullets dashed the Mercedes. The radiator punctured. The windscreen froze into a sheet of opaque ice, cracked, and wafted inwards, showering Deacon with glass. Blinded, he braked.

A single high-velocity bullet had passed through Ribbeck's chest, smashing his ribcage and ripping out his lungs and heart. Blood weltered the sedan's upholstery. Splashes and scrolls glistened wet red upon the side glasses. Deacon's shoulders and sleeves were soaked with it. SS Obergruppenführer Ribbeck had become a victim of Nazi ruthlessness and the Luftwaffe's skill. Flinching, Deacon recoiled from the corpse which had a hideous leer printed on the face and protuberant eyes from which hatred and anger had not quite faded.

Deacon punched shards of glass from the windscreen. He saw the fence, the lift of an earth dyke, scarf-like folds of the canal beyond. Opening the driver's door, hanging out, he looked back and forth. Caught in a kink in the road, the Mercedes was the only visible piece of traffic. That, Deacon thought, was the reason the dive-bombers had risked the strike; no fear of chopping up comrades in the panzer divisions.

The Mercedes crawled forwards.

Though Ribbeck was dead and the car damaged, they could still be of use.

Deacon tooled the car once more. Anxiously he scanned the canal dyke until he found a barge quay ramped up from the road. The engine coughed, steam hissed from the bonnet. There was just enough power left to gun the sedan up the ramp.

Deacon extricated himself and rolled out of the wide-open door as the Mercedes plunged over the edge of the quay into the canal, carrying the remains of Herr General Josef Ribbeck to a watery grave.

Deacon got to his feet and darted across the road into the sheltering trees.

Buz brought the ambulance along the road as fast as he dared. The important thing was to clear the farm track and pick up Deacon and Ribbeck without being spotted by the Germans. In spite of the size of the base camp and the ferocity of the Stuka attack, there appeared to be precious little activity on the road to the south. It was obvious, though, that decisions had been quickly taken, the Stuka pilots briefed to destroy the Merc, no matter if Obergruppenführer Ribbeck got it in the arse. Paget, it seemed, had also become dispensable.

Trolling the canal road, Buz hit the Granit's klaxon again and again. When he came to the barge quay, with its inviting ramp, he slowed the vehicle to walking pace. Sure enough, Deacon came high-balling out of the trees and flung himself through the canvas curtain.

Buz turned the Granit around, stopped it, parted the curtain behind the open cab, and asked, "All in one piece, lieutenant?"

"More or less, thank you, sergeant."

"Where's Ribbeck and the Merc? In the drink?"

"Absolutely."

"Stick on one of those German uniforms, lieutenant, and you can sit up front and give anybody who stops us a spiel in their own lingo, right?"

Deacon managed a grin. Kneeling, he unbuttoned his blood-soaked tunic.

A motorcycle combo shot past the ambulance. Buz kept his head and shoulders out of sight.

With Lisa's help Deacon was soon clad in a DRK uniform. It was anything but a perfect fit, tight in the crotch, short in the sleeves and with a collar like a hangman's rope. Deacon put on the forage-cap and clambered over the board into the Granit's cab.

"I'll try the other one for size," said Buz, "and join you in a minute. Meantime, I guess we should get moving."

"Past the encampment and over the bridge—bluffing all the way?" said Deacon.

"Yeah."

"How's Paget?"

"He is in great pain," said Lisa.

"Have you checked the medical supply box? There may be sedatives on board."

"No, there is nothing which will give relief."

Paget raised himself and said hoarsely, "Forget about me, please. Just do the best you can. But, lieutenant, remember your promise."

"Oh, that," said Deacon.

"You won't recant?"

Deacon's head was throbbing and he answered curtly. "No, I won't recant."

"With due respect, sir," said Buz Campbell, "hadn't we better push on?"

"Quite right," said Deacon, and turned his attention to the steering wheel.

They had nothing but coolness and courage to protect them now. With any luck, though, the Germans would still be searching for the Mercedes. Even after they found the hulk in the canal it would surely take them at least an hour to haul it out and learn that they had killed nobody except their own dear Obergruppenführer.

By then, Deacon hoped to be in or close to Bovet and the British fall-back lines. He would be vastly relieved to hand over the damned scientist to Major Holms, for Paget's despair was wearing on Deacon's nerves.

At a fast, steady pace Deacon drove the DRK vehicle north towards the Germans' pontoon bridge where his disguise and his command of the language would first come under scrutiny and be subjected to an acid test.

Capture now, Deacon knew, would mean torture and a firing-squad.

Progress towards the beach at Bovet was hardly easy. On the other hand, no serious challenge was made to the DRK vehicle. Ambulances were a familiar sight on the routes to the Front. Deacon managed to parry questions thrown at him by traffic control officers and by guards at the bridges it was necessary to cross. He was confident enough of his German to probe for information on the state of the British retreat. He learned that the BEF forces had indeed been pushed back to the Channel and were now engaged in a series of desperate holding actions while a flotilla of ships pulled the troops off the beaches.

"How's Holms going to find us?" Buz whispered.

"That's rather up to him," said Deacon. "Bovet is four miles north-east of Dunkirk, just beyond the Bray Dunes. It has a small, sand beach and a Mole and I expect Holms chose it for that reason.''

"What if Bovet's gone before we get there?"

"In that case we'll have to head into Dunkirk itself and fight for a place in a beach craft, try to make somebody in charge understand that Paget must have priority.''

"When do you think we'll get there?"

"At this rate, not much before six o'clock.''

"It's daylight until ten, close enough," said Buz. "That means the Jerry dive-bombers will have a field-day until the last kick.''

"Yes," said Deacon. "We're fortunate to be in a sector that the Germans have had time to clear. One must admire their efficiency. Look at the wreckage they've shifted already. It must have been a madhouse here yesterday.''

The reek of fuel mingled in the warm air with the sickening stench of death. Millions of pounds worth of equipment had been sacrificed by the retreating British army in its rush to the sea. Some of it, Deacon thought ruefully, had been issued from his own store only last week; he had probably signed the delivery chits himself. What an incredible waste! Off to the sides of the road, ammunition dumps blazed and the countryside was pitted with craters and the stumps of buildings. The most appalling spectacle of all, to the British soldiers in the ambulance, was a straggling column of Allied prisoners, ragged, dirty and dejected, being driven east by the Germans; a great jostling snake, several miles long, of soldiers who would spend the rest of the war in prison camps far from their loved ones and homes. It struck Deacon as ironic that so much effort had been made to save one man—Paget—when so many men had been sacrificed on the altar of inefficiency.

It was hours now since Deacon had eaten. He was glad to share the chocolate and bread that P.B. McNair produced from his sack of loot. The sticky meal was washed down with a mouthful of schnapps, and stale water from a canteen that Lisa had discovered in the rear of the ambulance.

Steadily, cautiously, Deacon navigated the thronged road. The DRK vehicle was given precedence at junctions and blocks, waved on in front of tanks and infantry carriers. Once he had got used to the crudity of its mechanics, the Granit was simple enough to operate and Deacon made few errors in handling. Tight-lipped, Buz sat upright beside him, sweating in the uncomfortable uniform.

In the rear, Paget was awake but, so Lisa whispered, comfortable enough after his cross-country ordeal. P.B., it seemed, had fallen asleep.

Sleep: it was thirty-eight hours since Deacon had rolled out of his camp bed in the RASC depot hut at Bovet. In that period he had performed more strenuous activity than he had done in months. But he did not feel weary. Not with the sea, with escape, drawing closer and closer with every passing mile. Buz, however, had been without sleep for much longer and the sergeant nodded and woke, drowsed and started throughout the interminable hour's ride into the village of Bovet.

There was a long delay at the Bovet bridge, the same one that Deacon had ridden over in the Matilda only twenty hours ago. The Matilda could hardly have been out of sight before the order had come through to abandon the position. The bridge had been blown by the Allies and promptly repaired by German advance parties. The country flanking it had been flooded by the demolition of a series of little dykes which kept the river from the flatland. Deacon assumed that the road to Bovet had been the scene of much fighting and confusion. He had missed all of that on the outward run, of course, having driven into the defended "corridor" at Quern.

"Ambulance," Deacon shouted.

He waved to attract the attention of a traffic control officer who was threading transports across the pontoon. Ditched vehicles were all around, some buried in soft mud up to the axles, a few overturned. Half-naked soldiers worked frantically at transferring howitzer shells from a foundered truck to the back of a half-track.

"Ambulance. Ambulance."

A zebra-stripped flag was waved at him by a German soldier in black uniform and white gauntlets.

Deacon nosed the Granit past two hooded artillery carriers and a forty-strong unit of grenadiers who, in marching order, looked as fresh and smart as if they had just been lifted from a toy-box. Crawling off the bridge end, scraping past the stone posts, was a monstrous 4 × 4 field-gun carrier. The zebra flag furiously signalled Deacon's ambulance into the vacant lot.

The traffic control officer was close to nervous collapse. He screamed at Deacon for his tardiness in obeying commands. Deacon apologized and brought the Granit abreast of the officer, a young and swarthy fellow, who continued to hurl abuse at the DRK men.

"Where are you from?" The officer pressed against the panel door, the flags in his hands like sabres.

"We're going to Bovet," said Deacon.

"What unit are you attached to?"

"DKR," said Deacon.

"Unit. Unit. Do you not understand plain German?"

"Do you not suppose," said Deacon, with just the right degree of insolence, "that you would do better to wave us through and let the grenadiers get on with winning the war?"

For a moment there was suspicion in the officer's eyes.

Deacon revved the Granit's engine.

He held his breath.

Beyond the bridge end he would be able to make a left fork, head out of the main column to the flanks of the village and enter territory that he knew quite well from his billeting there. The RASC depot had been situated only a half-mile away, under a pall of volcanic smoke that saturated the sky, which, quite probably, was all that remained of the temporary warehouses of his unit.

Buz too watched the traffic officer. Between his knees Buz held a Luger, loaded and ready to fire.

They were too far out yet to make a run for it.

At that moment, somewhere behind, an artillery captain shouted and the traffic control officer stepped back from the Granit's side and viciously snapped down his striped flag.

Deacon engaged gear and rolled the ambulance forward.

"Jesus!" murmured Buz.

"Amen," said Deacon, as he let his breath out.

Buz covered his mouth with his hand. "Which way to the beach?"

"Left," said Deacon. "It's about three miles to the coast road and the dunes. The Mole lies on the wing of the bay."

"Through the enemy lines?"

"I'm afraid so," said Deacon.

"Well, at least we haven't been rumbled so far."

"Amen again," said Deacon.

Seal-like, the head rose from the water. The trooper gasped, gulped in oxygen, and trod water. He had been down, Strumbannführer Staudt reckoned, for almost three minutes. To his left, and behind him, two more heads ripped the shiny gray surface of the Quern canal.

"Did you find it? Is the car there?" the Strumbannführer called out from the barge quay.

"Below. On mud," cried the first diver.

The Stuka pilots' report had been accurate after all. A message had been relayed to Staudt as he journeyed from St. Félice; the Mercedes had been intercepted, dive-bombed and driven into the Quern canal. Staudt had talked with the Stuka pilots by radio telephone and had managed to narrow the area of search. As there was no damage to the hedges along the mile of road that the Stukas had strafed, the barge quay provided an obvious starting point. Close inspection of the quay divulged fresh mud tracks. Staudt had sent down three volunteers, all strong swimmers.

"Are you sure it is the Obergruppenführer's Mercedes?" Staudt called out.

The swimmers stroked towards him.

Only then did he see the grisly trophies that they had collected and brought up from the wreck.

The men clung to the posts of the quay.

"This, sir," one said and reached up to hand Staudt the Oberguppenführer's pennant, torn from the bonnet mast.

"This, too," said a second swimmer, passing Staudt Ribbeck's cap, heavy with silver braid and canal water.

"How deep is the car?"

"Only fifteen feet below the surface."

"On a mud bank, sir."

"And," said Staudt, "how many people are inside it?"

"Only the Obergruppenführer."

"He is tied to the doorhandle, sir."

"God in Heaven!"

"Shot through the chest, sir."

"No other corpses?"

"None, sir."

"Come out." Staudt held the dripping cap in his hand. "You have done well."

"Shall we not bring the Obergruppenführer's body to the surface, sir? With ropes, it could—"

"That will not be necessary," Staudt said.

It would have to be done, of course, the Mercedes and the Obergruppenführer's corpse would have to be recovered. But he would set the engineers the task only after they had reopened the bridge at Quern which, he had been informed, would be within half an hour.

Staudt glanced at his watch, then at the sky.

Four hours until nightfall.

One corpse: Ribbeck's.

The English had escaped again. But they could not be too far ahead, not with a wounded man as cargo. It seemed unlikely that they would cross the canal here and go through Quern, an occupied town. It was more probable that they had chosen to hide in the nearby woods to wait for nightfall. But Staudt's guess was that the English radiers, who had shown themselves to be inventive and dedicated in the extreme, would have found some means of driving on towards the British lines. He would radio ahead, though he knew that he would receive no cooperation from the fighting officers at the battlefront. They had more to do with their time than be on the lookout for a party of escapers even if they had murdered an SS general.

With Ribbeck dead, however, Staudt could no longer afford to give up the chase. He must pursue them, try to pick up their trail before they reached the coast.

Turning on his heel, Staudt shouted, "Mauseberg, bring me my maps."

"What sectors?"

"Dunkirk, Bray Dunes and Bovet," Staudt replied.

* * *

The Mole at Bovet stuck two hundred yards out into the sea. A crescent of sand curved from the base of its inner wall, and tar-black herring sheds gave it root. Until yesterday afternoon its seaward abutment had been crowned by a handsome conical light in tusk-colored stone. But the pediment had been shaken by a Navy shell and was canted now at an acute angle, posing problems of balance for mystified seagulls that sought a perch on its ledges in the lulls between air-raids. The hanging threat of the Bovet light played on the nerves of Major Holms as he knelt in the bows of the fast twin-screw motor launch which was roped to the Mole's trawler rings below the low-water mark.

Registered under the unfortunate name of *White Feather*, the launch was the personal property of army captain Teddy Furnivall and had spent most of its sea life skittering about the Medway. Teddy's little fun ship was fast enough to put the wind up the drawers of the girls that he brought down from London, and comfortable enough in the cabin, which Teddy grandly referred to as "the ward room," to accommodate a couple in the horizontal position.

Teddy, thank God, was one of Division Four's thirty permanent members and had been "on tap" in the office in the Strand when Holms realized that the whole so-called rescue operation involving Paget had been undervalued and left, hopelessly, to a single Second Lieutenant, even if the lieutenant's name was Jeffrey Deacon and his pedigree as an adventurer impeccable.

"The Deacon, I say, you sent in the Deacon?" Teddy had crooned. "Our old Oxford muck-wallah; he who scaled the dizzy heights of Trinity tower in drear November with a mug of cocoa in one hand and—"

"Yes, Teddy; the same Deacon," Holms had interrupted.

"And he's somewhere in France liaising with your *amis* in a bold bid to shake this radio wizard loose from the talons of the Eagle?"

"Yes, Teddy."

"One chap?" Teddy had said, raising a sandy eyebrow. "Even such a chap as the Deacon? Is that all the wizard is worth?"

"I wasn't informed what Paget was worth until last night. Never mind the details, Teddy, they'll keep until later. The question is, how soon can you have the *Feather* fuelled and heading for France?"

"Oh you want the *Feather*, do you? What's wrong with the Royal Navy?"

"The harbors round Dunkirk are choked with sunken vessels and it's all small boats can do to get inshore. Apart from which, my arrangement is to rendezvous with Deacon at the Mole at Bovet at five p.m. tonight. I am rather pressed for time, you see."

"What if he doesn't show?"

"We'll wait."

"Dangerous," Teddy had said. "Very dangerous."

"I agree," Holms had said. "It's the sort of mess one expects when one is ordered to put together a unit which nobody knows exists and which is starved of equipment, manpower and proper training facilities."

"Peter, do you actually expect Deacon to turn up at Bovet, on time, in one piece, and dragging this radio genius home by the paw?"

"Frankly, no."

"Yet you must give every possible assistance, is that it?"

"Exactly. Now, about the *Feather*—?"

"What bell is it?"

"Ten minutes to two, a.m."

"If we shake a leg," Teddy had said, "we might just catch the morning tide."

"What will she carry?"

"Twenty at a pinch—including thee, me and Skipper Jones. He's an old sea-dog who looks after her for me. If he hasn't gone to Dunkirk already, I'm sure Jones'll pitch in."

"I've eight NCOs due any minute. They're coming from Dorset by truck."

"Due where?"

"The Armory in Cornhill Road."

"Eight NCOs! I see. You're dragging all our instructors along on this picnic?"

"Yes. Eight weapons instructors, plus two medics on loan from the RAMC."

"My, but you are taking this operation seriously, Peter."

"So, apparently, are the Germans."

"All rightee," Furnivall had said. "What are we waiting for? Put out the lights and let us depart."

The "heavy brigade" had duly arrived at the Armory and Teddy, driving his Aston, had led the truck to North Audley, a tiny village near Sheerness where the *Feather* was berthed. Skipper Jones, a grizzled fisherman, had had the launch fuelled and ready to depart.

In tranquil morning light, the party had set out across the Channel for the coast of France.

It had taken them the best part of ten hours to reach Bovet. The Channel was alive with vessels, large and small, the skies freckled with Luftwaffe fighters and counter-offence planes of the RAF. The beaches of Dunkirk were black with soldiers of the BEF, its harbor choked with crippled ships.

Bovet was no better. The bay's deep channel was blocked by the grounded hulk of a Royal Navy destroyer that had taken a direct hit and drifted in on the flood. A few tenders and lighters still plied out from the shore, ferrying soldiers from a mustering point by the herring sheds to larger vessels anchored offshore. But the evacuation from Bovet was almost over. Within an hour of the *Feather*'s arrival, the last British troops had taken to the boats and only a handful remained to support the French defence forces.

The village was defended against the claws of the panzer army by three French companies, a rearguard instructed to hold the line at all costs.

Holms watched the action through binoculars. In the dunes south of the herring sheds, the French had built hasty lines to keep back the German tanks. So far, the holding action had been successful. Evacuation continued from Bray Dunes and Dunkirk. But the Germans were regrouping in the north and northwestern sectors.

Given darkness and a dozen trained men, Holms could have wreaked havoc behind the enemy lines. As commander of Division Four, however, he had no choice but to observe the fighting from the deck of Teddy Furnivall's *White Feather*, watch and wait for Deacon.

Five o'clock came and went. Six o'clock, then seven.

The sky was no longer clear. Bands of clouds massed over the Channel and gathered inland. Dusk would come a little earlier than Holms had anticipated.

Culled from Division Four's Special Training Center, the eight NCOs were on deck too. Sprawling, they studied the battle as if it had been put on specially for their education. Teddy and Skipper Jones had gone below to catch some sleep.

Holms lowered his binoculars and rubbed his eyes with his knuckles.

It would be full dark in three hours. He would set a watch on the Mole as well as on the *Feather* and would catch forty winks then. Dawn would be at four. He expected a German assault then, a concerted raid on the French defences. There was no doubt in the major's mind that Bovet and its Mole would be in enemy hands soon.

After that, Deacon, poor sod, would have to fend for himself.

Raising the binoculars to his tired eyes once more, Major Holms scanned shore, village and promenade. He noticed, but did not particularly remark, a German Red Cross ambulance crawl along the skyline a mile beyond the French positions in the dunes. He had turned his attention elsewhere before the Granit ground to a halt.

DRK Senior Officer Roca Neff had joined the Nazi Party when he was sixteen years old. He would have wormed his way, somehow, into the Gestapo if it had not been for a wall-eye, an affliction which debarred him from élite departments in the Reich. Even his friends in the Hitler Youth Movement found the sight of Roca Neff pretty hard to stomach.

When war engulfed Europe, Neff, then twenty-six, grew a moustache, a jet black droplet, disguised his wall-eye with smoked glasses and used what pull he had to obtain a senior post in the German Red Cross. Of all Red Cross personnel in the war zone that day in early June 1940, only Roca Neff would have had the gall to take time off from his other duties to go in search of a missing ambulance.

Dielman and Heincke were special enemies of Neff. He suspected that the pair had taken off for an evening on the town, and promised himself he would find them and have their ears for ornaments.

It did not occur to Neff that Dielman and Heincke might be lying dead in a ditch or the Granit stuck in mud by the canal road. On paper, the Granit should have checked at Casualty Clearing Center No. 4 at 17.00 hours and the vicissitudes of war served as no excuse to Senior Officer Neff. He had had six mangled panzers to ship back to Quern and four of them had died on him, thanks to Dielman's and Heincke's desertion. Now he would be up half the night reordering his paperwork. Besides, the center was short of ambulances. Neff was mad, of course. He had been mad for several years. But nobody had noticed. Only madness would urge a man to bicycle out into the blitzed hinterland of Bovet in gathering dusk, risking snipers' bullets, mortar bombs, etcetera, to track down an ambulance that had probably gone up in smoke.

But that was Neff. Muttering, he crouched over the handlebars and pedalled along the secondary road, oblivious to tanks and half-tracks and panzers lying exhausted by the roadside, blind to everything that did not resemble a Granit ambulance.

It surprised him slightly when he actually found the missing vehicle. But there it was, crawling down the godforsaken road towards him, unlighted, unhurried and travelling in the wrong direction. Dielman and Heincke, the fornicators, had obviously stolen one of his precious vehicles to visit nurses in the inn at the Presteau crossroads, in neglect of their duties and to the detriment of his schedules. He would have them stripped of their rank, shot if possible.

Neff dismounted, pulled the bicycle across the center of the road and stood behind it, right arm raised, his gloved hand open, his gas-cape draped about him like a rubber toga.

The ambulance slowed and halted.

Neff may have been mad but he was not stupid.

He sensed at once that the driver was English. Certainly the massive man beside him had never been issued with such an ill-fitting uniform.

Smiling, Roca Neff approached the panel door.

"Are you lost, comrades?" he asked pleasantly.

"Yes, my friend," said the driver in passable German. "We have orders to pick up wounded from the Mole at Bovet."

A lie.

Neff kept smiling.

"Would you be kind enough to direct us to the Mole?" the driver asked.

Neff nodded. "Follow me. I will guide you."

"Clear of the guns, I hope."

"It is quiet now," said Neff affably. "You will be in no danger. Nobody fires on the Red Cross, not even the British."

"I wouldn't put it past them," said the driver.

Vaguely Neff wondered what had become of Dielman and Heincke. Had they been killed by this handsome imposter, this Englishman, and his giant companion?

"Come on then, we mustn't keep our brave wounded waiting," the driver said.

Shaking slightly under the gas-cape, Roca Neff straddled his bicycle and, glancing round, signalled the driver to follow him. Pedalling as hard as he could, he led the vehicle down the open road behind the duneland, towards the panzers.

"Something tells me not to trust this creep," Buz Campbell muttered.

"Odd," said Deacon. "I have exactly the same feeling."

"What do we do about it?"

"What do you suggest?"

"Knock him off the bike and run him over."

The ugly little German darted a glance over his shoulder, almost as if he sensed their intention. The bike wobbled. He held it grimly in balance and pumped the pedals, back arched.

Deacon hesitated.

It would be easy to wallop the chap with the Granit's bumper, tip him on to the grass verge and let P.B. take care of him. Unquestionably the little kraut was leading them back towards the German leaguers. Perhaps that was the only way to reach the promenade that linked Bovet, Bray Dunes and Dunkirk and gave access to the beach and the Mole. Certainly Deacon had found no through road, though he had been driving for twenty minutes.

"Uh-oh!" said Campbell. "I guess we left it too late."

Pushing the canvas curtain with his shoulder, the Canadian leaned backwards. "Waken up, wee man. We might be in for a scrap."

The panzer camp was visible from some way off, tanks bulked dark against the planes of a low white-painted building which Deacon identified as the Bovet Salt Water Spa. Tooling towards them along the road from the leaguer was a light truck containing four armed, helmeted German soldiers.

Deacon too leaned back against the canvas.

"Lisa," he said. "Keep Paget absolutely quiet."

"Yes, Jeff."

Agitatedly Campbell stirred beside him.

"It's now or never, lieutenant."

"Hold tight."

A moment before Deacon jumped the Granit forward, the kraut in the gas-cape began yelling, "*English spies. English spies. There, there. Take them. Take them.*" Raising his arms to gesticulate, he wobbled again and pitched headlong over the handlebars into the path of the German truck.

The truck, which had been cruising at no great speed, swerved and would have halted short of the sprawling DRK officer, but Deacon had already committed himself. The Granit's tires ground over the bicycle and squashed the body of the fallen DRK officer. The front bumper caught the lightweight patrol truck amidships. The ambulance bored on, thrusting the truck over on its side. Soldiers spilled out. Deacon would have driven through but Campbell hopped out of the Granit and, as he passed the tangle of the truck, Deacon saw the P.B. was already at work. He stopped the ambulance and reversed.

There were four shots, a brief rattle from an automatic weapon. Cries. Deacon sat at the wheel, not knowing what else to do, unable to bring himself to join the butchers by the roadside. A knife-blade glinted. A German wept for a split second before he died. Deacon looked away. When Campbell swarmed back over the side panel and dumped himself down in the seat, Deacon reached quickly for the ignition switch.

"We got them all," Buz Campbell said.

"Is P.B. with us?"

"Sure, sure. Drive, will you?"

They went on, steadily, down the long, exposed road behind the duneland and past the panzer leaguer.

It was after eight now and, on such a cloudy night, would be full dark by ten.

Deacon cleared his throat.

"I'm sorry, sergeant."

"Sorry for what?"

"Sorry I didn't help."

"It isn't your sort of job, lieutenant."

"What is my sort of job?"

"To get us out of this fucking town and on to the beach."

Deacon stiffened his failing nerve. "Of course."

"There must be a goddamned road somewhere."

"Oh, there is," said Deacon.

"Where?"

"Directly through the town center."

"And on to the beach?"

"On to the promenade; the promenade will take us to the Mole."

"Go that way," said Campbell.

"But if we're stopped," said Deacon, "we'll have no hope of escape."

"By morning, if you ask me, this entire stretch of coast'll be in German hands. Look at the fire-power they've stashed here. Think the Frogs'll hold for long against it?"

"You're right, Buz. You're absolutely right."

"No more back roads," Buz said.

"Straight through," said Deacon.

Buz wiped the knife-blade on his trouser leg and slipped it back into his belt. He had fired only one shot from the Luger yet the weapon reeked. The attack had been sudden, vicious and intimate. Buz felt strained. He told himself he needed sleep, sleep and hot food in his belly, told himself he should never have gotten mixed up with this officer and the cripple and the pretty French piece. P.B. and he could have been safe aboard a paddle-wheeler by now, steaming back to England. He knuckled his eyes. The cordite had stung them. One of the krauts in the truck had wept for his Ma before P.B. pushed a bayonet into his throat.

A hand appeared through the canvas, holding a bottle of schnapps.

Buz took the bottle and drank.

He watched the crowded German leaguer come towards them. Deacon drove slowly. Every goddamned instinct screamed for speed, but reason dictated otherwise. Buz drank again, fought the urge to belt down spirits until his senses were dulled and his reason impaired and he found relief from the ache in his bones.

He handed the bottle back to P.B.

On his right were faces, kraut faces, kids mostly. He could see them plainly. Blackout orders were not in force yet. Cigarettes glowed, and the soft blue glare of field cookers. He could smell hot stew, even through the rancid odor of burning oil and the pungent stench of shell powder. All of this sector was in German hands. Any poor British sucker who dragged his ass out of the hinterland would wind up a prisoner. Back towards Bray Dunes and Dunkirk, he suspected, there might still be ways open.

Deacon drove with his shoulders hunched, a pained expression on his features, like the tight uniform had shrunk tighter still.

The schnapps left an acid taste in Buz's mouth. He wanted a cigarette but he was scared to light one in case they drove on into a zone where the blackout restriction was being enforced and got stopped again. Christ, he wanted a cigarette so badly!

The ambulance swung past an ammo truck. Platoon commanders were drawing fresh supplies, to tone up the forward positions maybe. Buz had heard the pounding of big guns, seen aerial battles between Luftwaffe bombers and RAF fighters, had had sight of the harbors, polluted with burning oil and housing countless wrecks, one of which might well be the boat that Deacon's mysterious major had sent to collect them. If that was the case, there would be no hope for them, come morning.

Again the ambulance stopped; Military Police, German style. One cop shouted at Deacon who answered in a monosyllable.

Behind the MP stood the rubble of a hotel, the broken walls of residential houses. Up ahead, past a lorry laden with sand-tracks and wooden battens, infantry congregated. It struck Buz that he might have been wrong about the dawn attack. It smelled as if the krauts were lining up for a final assault on the French gun emplacements on the beach that night. Beyond the lorry and the assembling ranks he could just make out the scribble of waves on a sandy shore, the black, burned hulks of evacuation craft pounded by shore batteries and Heinkels.

The MP, a submachine gun tucked under his arm, came to the front of the Granit and bawled Deacon out.

Deacon answered curtly.

The Granit rolled back, Deacon working the gear stick, while the MP followed, slamming the bonnet with his fist.

Away across the sea the cloud-lid fissured, showing a butter-colored patch and the sun, still above the horizon, like a red ball. Behind the ambulance four half-tracks growled into the short street, one of them carelessly bringing down a fretted lamp-standard which crashed across the pavement and made the rear ranks of the infantry platoon leap away, cursing.

"Dear God!" Deacon said, under his breath.

Buz's stomach churned.

They were locked into the street now, surrounded by Germans.

The MP swung again, yelling.

Deacon simpered and jerked his thumb to point out that exit was blocked at the rear. The MP stalked up the side of the ambulance.

If he opens the rear flap, Buz thought, P.B. will knife him and we're all dead.

Desire for escape almost overwhelmed Buz. It would be easy to step down from the Granit, to walk across the rubble, to vanish. Jesus, if only they had thought to fix the canvas hood over the cab, maybe he wouldn't feel so fucking exposed.

Deacon shot him an enquiring glance.

Scowling, Buz shook his head.

Eighty yards up front, the German infantry platoon had gotten itself into formation and set up a low, vibrant song, muted but vigorous. Bullet-shaped helmets gleamed in the rays that leaked through the cloud. Far off to the left a massive explosion rocked the town; not a kraut head turned and the war-song went on without wavering.

"What's he doing back there?" Deacon hissed.

"Keep it quiet, for Chrissake," Buz snapped.

If the major *had* managed to bring a boat to the Mole, he would be lucky if he could hold it there for long. Perhaps there were pockets of resistance up the coast a ways and Dunkirk, in spite of the Luftwaffe, was still in Allied possession. But Bovet—Jesus, Bovet was strung like a bead on a wire. And the krauts were about to shear through that wire. Buz leaned over the door and looked back up the street.

Behind the half-tracks were personnel carriers, too many to count. He could feel the rumbling vibrations of heavy tanks, brought in, he guessed, from the leaguer on the north side of the bridge, fresh crews, rested and relaxed, the machines in good trim. Soon the beach would be flooded with German assault troops. Holding positions would be drowned by waves of panzers. Fight and fall back. Fight again, fall back; the pattern for the Allied troops was remorseless. He wished he was down there in the sand-pits with them, doing honest work, not stuck here sweating in a German uniform. Involuntarily he groaned.

"Steady," Deacon said. "Steady, old man."

The MP returned, calmer, though no more civil. He spoke German to Deacon for almost a minute, waving his arm. Deacon cut the engine. The MP tramped off towards the head of the column.

Deacon said, "Apparently, the British are moving men off the beaches only after dark. The Germans want to command position on the Bovet Mole to set up gun batteries. There isn't much hope of the Allies holding, so the MP says."

"What about us?"

"He thinks we're headed for Casualty Clearing Center number four, wherever that may be. We're to go out with the assault party, out of this street and turn right, run the gauntlet of Allied anti-tank guns for a couple of hundred yards, then turn into the town again."

"So what do we really do?"

"We certainly do not turn right," said Deacon. "We turn left on to the promenade and pray for a clear dash to the Mole."

"How far is it?"

"Two miles, at most."

"Jesus, lieutenant, I just hope your major's ready and waiting."

"He'd better be," said Deacon.

The proximity of battle stirred the SS Sturmbannführer's blood. His depression sloughed off as the beaches grew closer and the din of gunfire became constant. The fact that he was searching for the proverbial needle in this French haystack did not deter him. Staudt felt comfortable now, riding his armored car towards the battle-front. After driving over the pontoon bridge at Quern he had covered the distance to the hamlet of Bulshoek in a couple of hours with a dozen Totenkopf tanks and six personnel carriers rumbling majestically in his wake. He felt ridiculously happy for a major who had recently been party to an Obergruppenführer's death and who would, without doubt, be the subject of a stern military inquiry into the conduct of the St. Félice affair.

Mauseberg and Wester would probably not back him in the face of official rebuke. His one chance of avoiding an indelible slur upon his character as an officer of the Reich, and possible transfer to a grisly post as a concentration camp commandant, was to find the vanishing English raiders and the scientist, Paget. If he did not, he could at least commit the Totenkopf to the fighting and claim a measure of excuse—military exigency—to protect him from becoming a scapegoat for Ribbeck's stupidity. In fact, Staudt did not expect to track down his quarry. Only zeal, excitement directed him towards the dunes, leading his gallant little band of SS tanks.

As the rays of the westering sun broke through the cloud, Staudt's arm of vengeance found itself rolling on to the dunes on the occupied side of the Bovet Mole, approaching the Allied holding positions from the rear—as if it had been planned by high-ranking tacticians. The element of surprise caught the French and British off guard and, before he quite knew what was happening, SS Sturmbannführer Staudt was engaged in conducting a magnificent little action in the last hour of daylight against an enemy sapped by days of barrage and strung out in ill-prepared positions.

Deploying his tanks along the tussocky ridge above the stretch of "dirty" sand that linked Bovet to Bray Dunes Plage, Staudt braved the first uncoordinated rattle of fire from below.

Due south the sands were black with British soldiers awaiting pick-up from the beaches. Beachmasters were at the water's edge, checking out the improvised "piers," massing rowing boats and ferry craft in preparation for nightfall. Though Staudt suspected that the columns were out of range of the tanks' 38-inch guns, he directed Mauseberg to shell Bray Dunes, a shrewd piece of tactics that would make retreat along the sands doubly difficult for the soldiers below. Besides, the holding positions were probably too low, the PzKpfw IIs' dip angle and sand would muffle shell flak. Consequently, Staudt ordered an immediate six-tank barrage, using co-axial MG 34 machine guns and, with the Allied defences thus pinned, brought forth the Totenkopf's grenadiers.

There were a ferocious hand-picked crew from the regiment's best companies, the cream of which Mauseberg had selected for the St. Félice detail. Exultantly they took position behind the tanks. Cover was excellent. High-combed dunes, though only fifteen feet high above beach level, provided natural defence lines, with the added advantage that the soldiers in the scattered pits below had no means of gauging the depth of the force. In the dunes the Allied mortar emplacements had been constructed to hold against an attack from the north, from the Bovet-Bray Dunes promenade, a back-up to the main defence lines on the Bovet beach.

To the fortunate Staudt fell this prize.

He had four field mortars, a dozen tanks and eighty top-line grenadiers, SS trained, veterans of heavy fighting along the Maginot Line.

Staudt's unit could hardly fail to gain a victory.

It was all over in twenty minutes.

Desperate and courageous though the Allied troops might be, they had been caught off kilter from the flank. Those not killed, fled, emptying the gun pits in the sand and scuttling back towards the permanent defences of Bray Dunes Plage, abandoning the southern defence of the Bovet Mole.

Seventy-one French and British soldiers were taken prisoner, most of them walking wounded. The SS Totenkopf lost eleven men. Two of Mauseberg's tanks were partially damaged by anti-tank shells. One crew of three was severely wounded; a small price for a victory, all things considered.

The Sturmbannführer said as much during a telephone report to SS Gruppenführer Schauff, an old comrade, who was acting officer in command on the main fighting units of the Totenkopf 4th Division, now leaguered in the sector between Bovet and De Panne, five kilometres to the north. Staudt was requested to leave a company commander in charge of mopping-up and join the SS Gruppenführer in his field HQ at De Panne immediately. An attack against the Mole at Bovet and beach positions still held by the Allied rearguard was imminent. The Gruppenführer indicated that he would be proud to inform the general staff that a small unit of the Totenkopf had already put one claw in the enemy and made the way easier for the main attack force. Gratified and stimulated, Staudt crisply relayed the official orders to Mauseberg, then he mounted his armored car and, followed by two lightweight trucks, each carrying eight grenadiers, set out along the promenade towards Bovet.

It was Staudt's intention to skirt the town center and the Mole which, he thought, were not his concern. But Staudt miscalculated. The command car was still on the promenade when the attack began and the Granit ambulance, swinging left, broke off from the phalanx of fighting soldiers and bore down upon the major's little cavalcade.

Flagged right at the street's end by the MP, Deacon weaved the Granit across the ranks and swung left.

Angry shouts pursued him, but that was all. The establishing of forward assault positions and the flow of infantry and fighting vehicles was of much more importance to harrassed MPs than a rogue ambulance.

A wide street, debris-strewn, lay left. Façades of hotels and picturesque *pensions*, shops and restaurants shattered by shore guns and Royal Navy shells, caught the winey light, gold and blood-red planes made sharp by deepening shadows and drifting smoke. Ornate lamp-posts were bent and broken, the flattened stones below pitted and cratered. A fractured water-main had flooded the pavement and spread a lake across the space in which flower stalls had been set in summers past. The ambulance rushed across a corner of the water while Buz yelled advice and Deacon, head turtled between hunched shoulders, slid the big steering wheel through his fingers.

A white-painted wooden railing bordering municipal gardens had been almost demolished. Almond-shaped lawns and flower-beds churned to mud had become a graveyard for dozens of burned-out trucks abandoned by the Allies. The end wall of the gardens was piled with metal junk, a "stand" vacated only an hour ago.

Deacon braked, braked again and cautiously manoeuvred the Granit through the wrecks towards the promenade.

Behind and to the right, German tanks prowled towards the beach, a thumbnail of white sand where, in better days, well-to-do French families had sunned themselves, nicely removed from the fishy odors of the Mole and its herring sheds. Out in the bay the carcasses of Royal Naval vessels heeled on the ebb tide, gigantic, rusting already in the salt air, keels holed and super-structures bombed. Nothing was on the move within the arms of the bay, no skoots, lighters, pinnaces or motor launches.

"Can you see anything that might be Holms' boat?"

"Not a goddamned thing," Buz answered.

Deacon felt betrayed. He cursed Holmes and the bunglers in Division Four at the top of his voice.

The ambulance jarred over a shallow ditch and stone coping on to the promenade and veered left again.

The broadwalk had been cleared of most of its debris. Only the dross of that day's fighting remained, corpses mostly, like old meal sacks draped across the iron rails or crouched in improvised emplacements, heads lolling and arms outflung.

One dark hole, like a bite made by teeth, was torn out of the promenade. A Berliet anti-aircraft gun carriage with a broken back had been tipped into it. The decapitated body of a French gunner was spiked on the mangled rail. The sun's rays, piercing bruised blue cloud, turned everything to bronze and the tableau of death had a posed, monumental quality that diminished its horror.

"Can you see the bloody Mole yet?" Deacon shouted.

"Yeah."

"And a boat?"

"No, no boat."

"Oh, for God's sake! It *must* be there."

"What's that?" Buz cried. "Dead ahead of us. Christ! It's a German patrol."

"Get the guns, Buz. Get P.B. up front."

"No, we've fooled the krauts already," Buz shouted. "We can fool them again. Ride on through."

"What if they've found the cyclist?"

"Slow down and ride through easy like. Don't blow it now."

Deacon braked and steered the Granit's tires perilously close to the edge of the promenade. The three German vehicles had been strung out abreast but, identifying Red Cross markings, pulled right and slowed too.

The Mole was less than a mile off, hidden for most of its length by the prow of a sunken coaster. On the beach a French gun-crew was dashing across the shallows pursued by machine-gun fire. The Granit moved into the inside slot. No way but forward. No way but straight along the pitted promenade or down one of the concrete donkey ramps to the sand.

Buz gripped Deacon's shoulder. "Keep it going, lieutenant, just keep it going."

The SS Sturmbannführer rose up from the command car like an apparition.

Standing erect, hands on the windscreen of the open cab, Staudt gaped in disbelief at the slow-moving ambulance and the tall figure in DRK uniform.

"God in Heaven!" Staudt exclaimed. "That's the sergeant we took prisoner this morning."

"Jesus, that rips it!" said Buz Campbell who, at precisely the same moment, had identified Staudt.

Above the roar of the Granit's engine, the Sturmbannführer's command was inaudible. The SS troopers response was immediate, however.

The truck halted and emptied.

The ambulance was adjacent to, then past the group before Deacon heard the concentrated clatter of gunfire. He flung his weight against the wheel and the Granit left the flat promenade and plunged down one of the donkey ramps into the rim of soft, undampened sand against the sea-wall.

From the back aperture P.B. was blasting away. Three kraut vehicles were visible, swung into position at the edge of the wall, then one vanished, swung back into view and found the ramp.

Soft pouting sand clung to the Granit's wheels as it catapulted on to the beach.

Deacon lost control.

The ambulance lurched, swayed, listed hard right and, as Deacon groped for the handbrake, went over.

Pitched clear, Deacon squirmed and hauled at the sand to pull himself clear of the Granit though the vehicle was already on its side. P.B., who seemed immune to crises, was already on his knees behind it pumping the Lee Enfield.

Like the ambulance, the panzer truck struck the sand at the wrong angle, keeled over and crashed on to its side. A couple of soldiers were trapped beneath it. The driver's arm was pinned by the door of the cab, and his screams of agony overlaid the sounds of shooting.

So far only one gun, McNair's, had been fired. The *pang-pang-pang* of the Lee Enfield echoed from the sea-wall. Germans scrambled for cover. At a range of thirty yards, however, the Scot's tally was high. No shot had yet been directed at Deacon, P.B. or the Granit.

Deacon ran to the ambulance and whipped up the flap.

Lisa, though dazed, was unhurt and already pulling Paget towards the opening. Buz had jumped clear of the cab before impact and had reached the rear a split-second after Deacon. Deacon ducked as a stream of machine-gun bullets plucked holes in the canvas overhead.

"Is Paget alive, Lisa?"

"Yes, yes," the girl cried. "He has passed out, that is all."

"Grenades, wee man," Buz said. "Use the grenades."

More than schnapps had been stored in P.B.'s loot sack. Deacon flung himself on top of Lisa and Paget in the mouth of the awning as two almost simultaneous explosions rocked the Granit. The machine gun's stammer ceased. Debris showered the awning followed by a rush of sand and the fat soft detonation of the panzer truck's gas tank.

"For Chrissake," Buz bellowed, "pull Paget clear."

Deacon grabbed the unconscious man by the thighs, hauled him along the canvas and over the tailgate. Buz took the weight, eased the scientist down on to the sand and dragged him behind the overturned Granit.

P.B. was off to the left, rifle tucked under his arm, his hand to his mouth. For an instant, daftly, Deacon imagined that P.B. was sucking his thumb. Then he saw a third grenade, black and small in the air and watched its parabola as it curved high on to the promenade. On all fours on the sand, he covered Paget once more. Buz hugged Lisa against his chest.

Blast swept a carpet of sand across the edge of the broadwalk. Loose stones dumped around Deacon. He squinted through the smoke at the rake of the promenade, saw kneeling troopers and squirts of flame as semi-automatics opened fire. They were pinned down and vulnerable. Even P.B. could hardly shoot them out of this one. The advantage of high ground, the promenade, belonged to the German major and his panzers. Very soon a vanguard of German assault troops would pour south from Bovet center.

Releasing Lisa, Buz pulled Deacon down and thrust his mouth to his ear.

"I'm going for the Mole," Buz said. "I'm taking your goddamned scientist with me. Give me covering fire, right?"

"All right." Deacon patted Buz on the side of the jaw. "We'll hold as long as we can."

The foundered German truck was burning furiously. Veils of choking smoke fanned out on an offshore breeze, Deacon loaded the Webley. His hands, he noticed, were steady. Beside him, kneeling too, Lisa held a Luger in both fists. She glanced at Deacon and smiled. There was nothing arch in it, nothing silly or sentimental. She was saying goodbye.

Stooping, Buz pushed his arms under Paget, found a comfortable hold and rose, lifting his burden. Screened by smoke drift, the Canadian lumbered off with the injured scientist in his arms. Only yards from the protection of the Granit, Buz stumbled, paused and slung Paget over his shoulder. Dipping, Buz went on again towards the sea.

With discrimination, Lisa fired the Luger. Rhythmically she swung her body around the Granit's vertical tailgate and tugged the trigger, slender arms recoiling, then swung back as the angry chatter of German guns replied from the promenade. Deacon reached over her, aimed, and shot single rounds from the Webley. Their fire-power was woefully inadequate. One grenade would wipe them out. He waited for it, oblivious to the noise of battle that vibrated down the beach, to the thunderous sounds of big combat, mortars against tanks, shells against armor and a constant medley of machine guns. One minute dovetailed into another. He felt as if he was hanging unfairly on to life—and went on squeezing single rounds from the Webley. When P.B. crabbed round the corner of the canvas hood, Deacon almost shot him through the head. The Scot dived flat and, under a rain of bullets from the promenade, squirmed into cover. In one hand he carried a Bren and the weight of the loot sack, slung carelessly about his neck, was obvious.

"Here, see what I found?" The corporal dropped the Bren on the sand at Deacon's feet.

"Where did—?"

"Down the beach."

"Buz?"

"On his way," said P.B. "Best get the lassie out'f here, eh?"

Until that moment it had not occurred to Deacon that he was in some measure responsible for Lisa. The focus of his attention had been Paget. But Paget was gone now and Buz had had ample time to clear the site.

"Got these an' all." P.B. flipped open the haversack and showed Deacon five stick grenades, like ugly lollipops. "Head straight for the water. There's two wee foxholes down there."

P.B. was already in a firing position, belly down, the Bren thrust out before him.

The first burst from the Bren drowned Deacon's shout.

He caught the girl by the arm, hauled her from cover and weaved away from the Granit, retreating across open beach towards the edge of the sea.

Almost before Deacon knew what was happening, he fell into the first of the deep sand holes, Lisa on top of him. Shored with planking, the hole had been shelled. The mangled corpse of a French infantry corporal cowered against the boards. Personal equipment was scattered round, ration tins and the empty water canteens. It was a foul place and Deacon's senses recoiled. He was ashamed of having brought Lisa here and would have pulled her on towards the sea if she had not stayed him. P.B. too was retreating. Barely ten yards from the ambulance when it blew up, the corporal flattened himself on the sand for a few seconds then ran straight towards the foxhole and flung himself over the lip.

"They're comin'," P.B. panted, "along the beach. The brass-hat's car. An' two fuckin' tanks."

Deacon popped his head up. He could see on to the promenade now. The bodies of seven or eight panzers were spread about the wreckage of a truck.

"Right'n the bloody button," McNair chuckled.

Two light tanks from the German attack had found hard sand and were prowling towards them, led by the fast-moving armored command car.

"There's a boat, though," said McNair.

"Where?"

"Comin' round."

"Where?"

"Out there."

So Holms hadn't let him down after all.

The motor launch purred down the length of the coaster's prow, hugging it, diminutive against the seagoing vessel's plates. On its deck Deacon glimpsed an armed force, smart as paint in combat rig. He felt—almost—like cheering.

The PzKpfw's first shell shuddered overhead, crumped into the sand thirty yards away and put paid to the lieutenant's jubilation. A second shell erected a column of sand between the foxhole and the sea, obliterating sight of the rescue launch.

The beach shuddered and the bloody corpse of the French corporal slumped sideways as if instinct to duck at the sound of shells remained strong even after death.

"The next one'll be on target," Deacon yelled. "Clear out."

P.B. stood up. The motion of his arm was almost too swift to be visible—a long pull-back, uncoiling, a release. The movement was repeated. In the air two stick grenades twirled. They fell short of the tanks but showered the approaching command car with sand. The car swerved. Deacon swarmed over the lip of the hole and, dragging Lisa behind him, headed for the sea.

Held hard against his hip, P.B. swept the Bren in a narrow arc as the Sturmbannführer's car emerged from the curtain of sand. Blinded, the driver fought to regain control, snaking and swerving while P.B. strafed the vehicle.

The tanks fired again.

Deacon went belly down, Lisa beside him.

Shells sang overhead and pummelled the beach.

Ten yards in front of the lieutenant a hummock of oil drums marked the last foxhole above the flood-tide line. In the aftermath of tank fire, Deacon could barely make out the sea and could not see the motor launch at all. He yanked Lisa to her feet and headed for the hole. The girl sobbed, winded by the blasts and the mad dash down the beach. Deacon's head buzzed, his ears whined, his skin felt as if it had been flayed from the bones of his face. It was all he could do to stagger to the oil-drum redoubt, with Lisa clinging to his arm, and tumble over the edge.

Campbell and Paget lay against the shallow sand slope, the scientist, conscious now, propped against empty ammo boxes.

Blood darkened Buz Campbell's shoulder and dripped stickily down his left arm. His bluff features had turned waxy with loss of blood.

"The krauts have the Mole," he said. "No rescue boat."

"Yes, in the bay," said Deacon. "How badly are you wounded?"

Shrapnel in the shoulder. Maybe the bone's gone."

"Can you walk?"

"Yeah, sure. But I can't carry his nibs any more."

"*Do it, lieutenant*," Paget suddenly screamed. "*Keep your promise. Shoot me. Shoot me.*"

"For Chrissake, shut your mouth," Buz snapped.

"*Please, please, lieutenant.*"

On her knees, Lisa spoke softly to the man. Paget's terror had overridden pain. He was animated by fear. Whatever committee had selected Paget for such a mission should have been strung from the yardarm. The scientist beckoned pathetically. "Please, do it. I'll close my eyes. Don't let them take me."

"SHUT IT."

Paget fell silent.

Crawling to the edge of the hole, Deacon surveyed the beach.

For some reason the tanks had stopped sixty or seventy yards away. In slanted light, amid smoke, judgement of distance was impossible. Behind the tanks German infantry soldiers were strung along the beach. More foot soldiers were running along the promenade. The last Allied resistance, it seemed, had crumpled.

The crinkle of the high-tide line was only twenty feet from the lip of the foxhole. Beyond it a dipping slope of packed sand ran thirty yards into the sea. Out in the bay wrecked vessels looked like sets from a Wagnerian opera, dwarfing the launch as it nosed out of the channel between the coaster's prow and a sunken mine-layer.

Deacon waved his arms and drew a hail of fire from his right. Swivelling, he saw the command car roaring down on them, its MG blazing. He watched a grenade roll lazily across the sand. The command car roared over it—then lifted—then reared up. P.B. sprinted out of the smoke.

At the same moment the motor launch sounded its klaxon, a comical *whoop-whoop*, shrill enough to pierce the bedlam of the guns.

P.B. flung himself over the oil drums and rolled, unharmed, into the hole. From the smoking hulk of the command car an SS major stumbled.

From the promenade panzers poured on to the beach.

The klaxon whooped invitingly.

Deacon gripped Paget and hoisted him up. He was no light-weight. Deacon staggered, found balance and, with the scientist hanging across his shoulder, quit the foxhole and began an interminable trudging run towards the water.

At any instant Deacon expected to be shot. He hugged Paget's legs with both arms. Draped across him, hands gripping Deacon's belt, Paget's peevish voice raved on.

Cold water encased Deacon's calves. He hoisted Paget higher, wading out. The water felt heavy, like mercury. He was crotch-deep before he took his feet from the bottom and wallowed over. Paget's voice gurgled into silence then spluttered and choked out more protests as he surfaced. By now Deacon was indifferent to danger. He snared Paget's flailing arms and jerked the man to him, laying his body, belly to back, under Paget's. He let the sea take him. It was a relief not to be upright any more. He could hardly believe that he had made it. He kicked his legs, thrusting. He stared up at the sky. It was powder-blue and violet, streaked with carmine; a large poetic sky, Deacon thought, stroking, relieved that Paget had had the wit to cease his struggles. Held above water, the man's head bounced on Deacon's chest, arms dragging like fins.

When other heads came past him, Deacon was rather surprised. He saw them, only yards away, their noses pointed landward, semi-automatic rifles held high in the ungainly position in which he too had been taught to raid a beach, back in dear old Dorset. He recognized Patterson, a weapons instructor. And Kemp, a maniac for physical conditioning. And Staffy Clarke. They bobbed past him, giving him a wink and a nod, as if to say "good chap." Then there were heads at his side, hands plucking at him. He looked over his shoulder, twisting, saw the reflections of water on the varnish of the motor launch, and Teddy Furnivall, chuckling, hanging from a rope, reaching to lend him a hand.

"Cautiously, old boy. With due care and attention." Teddy told him. "Mustn't have you pipped on the post."

Then more hands took away the weights that had mysteriously become attached to his legs and, as Deacon shed the water, he shed all cares and all burdens too and, lightly, passed out.

Dressed in warm, dry clothing from Teddy's slop chest, Deacon joined Lisa and Major Holms in the tiny for'ard cabin. It was after eleven and the night was like velvet as the launch, steered by grizzled Skipper Jones, weaved across the English Channel.

"Where are the others?" Deacon asked.

"All safe and comparatively sound," Peter Holms told him. "We managed to pull them off the beach. No fatalities, though your *bête noire* from Dorset, Sergeant Kemp, collected a bullet in the leg."

"And Campbell?"

"The Canadian? Oh, he's weak from loss of blood but our

medics will patch him up. His wounds aren't serious. Couple of weeks in a hospital and a month's convalescence should see him right. Where, in God's name, did you pick up such a pair of heroes?"

"I found them in Quern."

"They were prepared to die in that foxhole, Jeff, to cover your escape."

"Oh, yes." Deacon accepted the glass of whisky and water that Holms poured for him. "They're courageous all right. Perhaps a little mad, but in the best possible way. How's Paget?"

"Under sedation."

Deacon sipped whisky. It made him feel sleepy again. He calculated that he had been "out" for over an hour, poleaxed by exhaustion and nervous strain.

Deacon said, "It was a cock-up, sir. From start to finish, a complete cock-up."

"I'm only too well aware of it," Holms said.

"I expect you'll require a full report?"

"Of course."

"I don't intend to pull any punches," said Deacon.

"I wouldn't expect you to," said Holms. "I'll be delighted to present your report, uncensored, to the next Defence Department subcommittee meeting. If the powers-that-be really do want a special sort of service, then they'll have to be prepared to back it to the hilt."

"I'm not terribly interested in politics at this moment," said Deacon wearily. "If I had known what a makeshift division we were, I'd never had volunteered. I tell you, sir, if it wasn't for the French partisans in St. Félice, your Mr. Paget would be in the hands of the Gestapo by now."

Deacon put his hand on Lisa's shoulder. She too had been given dry clothes. She sat close to Deacon now, her knees touching his. Her eyes were luminous in the shaded lamplight, her face very pale.

Deacon said softly, "You have your friends in France to thank for the success of this ridiculous operation."

"Yes, I know," said Holms. "How high was the cost?"

"Too high," said Deacon.

He covered Lisa's hand with his.

"Is it safe to go on deck?" he asked.

"Oh, yes," said Holms. "But no lights, hm?"

Deacon's legs were like lead. His body ached. He had never before felt so thoroughly defeated. Relief had not been replaced by triumph. Too many images flew about in his memory. Too many parts of the tale had still to be told. Followed by the French girl, he climbed the ladder.

It was cold on deck. At the stern, wrapped in blankets, the "heavy brigade" slept.

Deacon led Lisa forward and leaned against the high, spidery railing, looking down at the waves that the bow split from the dark sea. All along the coast of France, tracers flickered and the sheet-lightning glare of howitzers lit the sky. The fluctuating glow of many fires showed on the belly of night clouds, and the grumble of guns came loud across the water.

He put his arm about Lisa's shoulders.

All around, he could sense the presence of other small craft; the evacuation flotilla. He could discern the unlit bulk of a Royal Naval vessel, low and raffish on the waterline, and the mellow churn of her screws as they powered her south-east, heading for Dunkirk.

Lisa said, "I must go back soon, Jeff, back to France."

"Why, Lisa?"

"My father is there. He will need me. I can be of use again."

"Of use?"

"In fighting this war."

"What if—what if—?"

This was the hard part, the ugly part, the moment to which he had been travelling and which had tainted the pleasure of a victory against the odds. Now he had to tell her the truth, hand her loneliness and grief, the Obergruppenführer's damned awful legacy.

The salt sea air smelled so clean.

She was soft against him, Lisa Vandeleur, a girl he had loved long ago in another country before war had changed him, changed everything.

He hated being the stranger who must tell her the news that her father had died in St. Félice.

"What is it, Jeff? What's wrong?"

Deacon took a deep breath.

"Listen," he said.

6 Special Air Service

CAIRO HAD BEEN ONE LONG, drunken debauch and Deacon left for the desert with a feeling of relief, plus the father and mother of all hangovers.

It was many months since he had returned from Bovet on Furnivall's *White Feather*. After a blazing row with Major Holms, he had been posted to a Central Supplies Unit which, in due course, had carried him on its coat-tails to the Middle East. Since then Deacon had almost forgotten that Division Four existed and that he was still, officially, part of it.

When he was sober, which wasn't too often, Deacon sometimes regretted his outburst at the High Command's handling of the St. Félice rescue, and his adamant refusal to sing dumb. He had demanded a hearing before the Special Operations Committee and had torn into them with passion and vehemence, qualities that military authorities did not encourage in young subalterns. Campbell and McNair had not been summoned to appear before the committee and Lisa, by then, had been returned to Paris. Holms and Furnivall had been notable by their absence and Deacon had been left to make a fool of himself, alone.

What galled Deacon more than anything was that Lisa seemed to blame him for what had happened in St. Félice and, by inference, for the deaths of her father and friends. There was absolutely no logic to the accusation, yet Deacon smarted under it and felt guilt instead of pride at his part in Paget's rescue from the hands of the enemy. Naturally, he got no thanks from Paget. He never saw the man again and shed no tears over that. He had visited Campbell once in the hospital, a week after their return to England but had soon lost touch with the Canadian who, with

McNair, had been sent back to the Royal Langhams, a regiment not involved in the desert war.

Deacon's punishment of speaking his mind had not been subtle. He had been dumped in Central Supplies to sit out the duration of the war or die of booze or boredom.

The first the lieutenant knew of the formation of a new regiment, apart from idiotic rumors circulating in the mess, was when he received a standard cable from Holms.

The cable said: *Division Four has been disbanded. You have been transferred to the 1st Special Air Service Regiment and will be required to undergo immediate advanced training. You will be collected at 16.00 hours today.*

Cynic and sceptic, Deacon did not believe a word of it. He spent the afternoon drinking in the bar of the Continental but elected, at the last moment, to show up with his valise and suitcase outside the Supplies mess. He was somewhat less than steady on his feet and weaved a little as the three-ton truck pulled round from the guardhouse and drew up by the mess steps.

"Deacon?"

The driver was a lieutenant too; his complexion was burned black by desert sun and he wore a lard-like lip salve which made him look, Deacon thought, like Al Jolson.

"Ah, so you found me," Deacon said.

"Stow your gear and hop in."

"Where are we headed?"

"Kabrit."

"Where's that?"

The driver did not answer.

Deacon climbed aboard and the truck took off in a flurry of dust.

The driver did not deign to answer any of Deacon's questions during the ride out. Deacon eventually fell asleep.

When he wakened, the truck had stopped before a row of tents on the edge of a waste of brown sand. It was almost dark but the desert twilight backlit a series of gigantic scaffolds that Deacon recognized as parachute jumps. He had received training on similar structures back in Ringway before making the six regulation drops that he needed for his parachute wings. The very sight of the damned helter-skelters made him tense. He struggled to get out of the cab, but the driver was back before Deacon got to the ground.

"Stay put. You're wanted elsewhere."

"Where?"

"Up country."

"Oh!"

Deacon settled back into his seat.

An hour out from Kabrit he fell asleep again.

It was pitch dark and bitter cold when he came round again. He felt awful. His head thumped and his stomach moiled and he was in sore need of a large mug of tea, his usual medicine after a skinful. He checked his wristwatch and found that it was close to midnight. At the rate the truck was shifting, over a sand track at that, he fancied they must be a hundred miles from Kabrit by now.

"Not lost, are we?"

"No," the driver growled.

Twenty minutes later, to Deacon's vast relief, the three-tonner slowed and crawled to a halt before a low-slung marquee surrounded by six or eight ridge-tents. In the faint glow of the headlamps Deacon caught sight of a fuel dump, netted and camouflaged. The driver killed the blackout lights.

"You're here. Out."

Deacon got out. The driver slung his valise and suitcase after him, turned the truck and headed back into the night.

Deacon's mouth was pursed with thirst and he looked forward to the welcome, the inevitable whisky-and-soda or mug of tea that would be offered him by the OC of this far-flung unit, the hospitable gestures of gentlemen maintained even in primitive places, that old diehard colonial spirit.

But the tents remained dark and deserted.

Instinct told Deacon that he had better wait right where he had been put, and not go prowling in search of company.

Ten minutes passed, a quarter of an hour.

Deacon shivered. The night air was cold as ice, whipped by a rising breeze that seemed to stream out of infinity.

When the plane came over, the sound was frightening, sudden and thunderous and very close over the lieutenant's throbbing head. Involuntarily Deacon threw himself to the ground. The transport craft zoomed over him, dust and sand sucked up by its props. Deacon remained face down, listening to the cut of the Pegasus engines and howl of brakes, the sounds of a landing not far off. Only when the plane was silent did he push himself to his feet.

Another five minutes passed and then, out of the darkness, a familiar voice shouted, "This way, sir. Step lively."

Deacon stooped to lift his baggage.

"No room for those, lieutenant," said Sergeant Campbell. "Won't be needing your pajamas tonight, right?"

"What are we on, sergeant?"

"Night drops."

"Where's the plane?"

"Half a mile."

"Which way, for God's sake?"

"Thataway. Follow me, and don't get lost."

"On the double?"

"Always on the double," Buz Campbell said. "It's an SAS trademark."

The dry mouth, the dirty remnants of the hangover were forgotten. Deacon's legs trembled at the effort of trotting through the sand, and his eyes watered at the sting of the abrasive wind. But he was beginning to feel clean again, to find a germ of pride. He was no fool; he knew what was coming and he welcomed it, a dangerous night drop out of some ancient aircraft. The hairy tales he had heard of Colonel Stirling's SAS squadrons were beginning to shape up as true. Besides, there was Campbell; tighter, fitter, less garrulous, but as steadfast as ever.

"How's the arm?" Deacon panted.

"Healed fine."

"How long have you been here?"

"Couple of days here. With the squadron, five months."

"Did Holms muster you out of the Langhams?"

"Somebody did. Yeah, probably Holms."

"And McNair?"

"On board."

"I suspected as much."

"Save your breath, lieutenant. You'll need it."

The plane was a Bristol Bombay troop transporter, not the best machine in the world from which to parachute, but not the worst either. Buz Campbell bundled Deacon inside. The first thing the lieutenant saw, by the faint light of a safety lamp, was P.B. McNair's simian grin. He grinned back.

McNair was one of eight men already braced inside the Bombay's belly. All wore X-type harnesses rigged, Deacon noticed, to the Bombay's fixed seats, which was no place for static lines really, but seemed, somehow, to typify the ethos of the mob that he had fallen into.

Buz handed him a pack.

"Remember how it fits?"

"Of course," said Deacon, fumbling.

Buz helped him, clipped the static line into the chair runner and sorted out his own parachute. Seated, legs thrust out, Buz shouted and the Bristol Bombay roared and manoeuvred for take-off along a desert strip lit only by small flares which would be extinguished immediately after the plane was in the air.

P.B. tapped Deacon's arm and passed him a gill bottle of whisky which was already half empty. Deacon took a mouthful, returned the gill and hung on as the Bombay taxied along rutted ground and hoisted itself laboriously into the air.

Behind and to his left there was a hole in the floor; the exit. It was unhatched during the brief flight and the air in the back of the plane was like liquid oxygen. Deacon's lips turned numb. Buz handed him a woollen balaclava that smelled of mutton fat. No smock, no heavy boots, no special helmet; just the balaclava to keep the wind from whistling in one ear and out the other.

Leaning, Buz shouted, "We send out a 'stick'—ten men—in fifteen seconds. The major's down there, somewhere in the dropping zone, and if we don't do it right we fly again until we do."

"What about the wind?"

"What wind?"

"Dear God!" said Deacon.

"You ain't scared, lieutenant?"

"Of course I'm scared."

"Remember St. Félice."

"I'd rather not, thanks."

"Some chicken-shit operation that was," said Buz at the top of his voice. "If it hadn't been for us—"

"That was yesterday," Deacon said. "I'm more concerned about tomorrow."

"The real stuff," Buz shouted. "Oh, yeah! The real stuff. Lieutenant, you ain't seen nothing yet."

On the wall of the fuselage the red light went out and a green bulb glowed.

Buz signalled.

Deacon crawled to the rim of the exit hatch and rose, unsteadily, to his feet.

Buz pointed downward into the darkness. "Only fifteen hundred feet. Flat sand. No lights. Keep your eye peeled. Don't land on our trucks. You ready?"

"Yes—but is this necessary?"

"Jesus!" said Buz Campbell and thrust Deacon in the small of the back with his knee.

Compact and upright, Deacon shot down into the air. He knew the exit was fine and waited, still falling, for the canopy to develop, letting his breath out in a long sigh as the lines snapped and his body lifted a little and the descent became controlled by wind drift.

The wind was high, though, and he skimmed left. It didn't worry him. Above, other parachutes bloomed. He heard the roar of the Bombay diminish into a drone. Wind hissed in the lines and then, from not far off, Deacon heard Campbell singing, the same crazy song he had sung all those months ago on the road to St. Félice.

And Deacon sang too, at the top of his voice, all the way down to the desert floor.

Watch for

MAILED FIST

next in THE FIGHTING SAGA OF THE SAS series
from Pinnacle Books

coming in July!

LEWIS PERDUE

THE TESLA BEQUEST
A secret society of powerful men have stolen the late Nikola
Tesla's plans for a doomsday weapon; they are just one step away
from ruling the world.
☐ 42027-7 THE TESLA BEQUEST $3.50

THE DELPHI BETRAYAL
From the depths of a small, windowless room in the bowels of
the White House, an awesome conspiracy to create economic
chaos and bring the entire world to its knees is unleashed.
☐ 41728-4 THE DELPHI BETRAYAL $2.95

QUEENS GATE RECKONING
A wounded CIA operative and a defecting Soviet ballerina hurtle
toward the hour of reckoning as they race the clock to circum-
vent twin assassinations that will explode the balance of power.
☐ 41436-6 QUEENS GATE RECKONING $3.50

THE DA VINCI LEGACY
A famous Da Vinci whiz, Curtis Davis, tries to uncover the truth
behind the missing pages of an ancient manuscript which could
tip the balance of world power toward whoever possesses it.
☐ 41762-4 THE DA VINCI LEGACY $3.50